HER GENEROUS BILLIONAIRE

JULIETTE DUNCAN

BILLIONAIRES WITH HEART CHRISTIAN ROMANCE

Cover Design by http://www.StunningBookCovers.com

Copyright © 2019 Juliette Duncan

FOREWORD

HELLO! Thank you for choosing to read this book - I hope you enjoy it! Please note this story is set in Australia. Australian spelling and terminology have been used and are not typos!

As a thank you for reading this book, I'd like to offer you a FREE GIFT. That's right - my FREE novella, "Hank and Sarah - A Love Story" is available exclusively to my newsletter subscribers. Go to http://www.julietteduncan.com/subscribe to get the ebook for FREE, and to be notified of future releases.

I hope you enjoy both books! Have a wonderful day!

Juliette

CHAPTER 1

Sydney, Australia

The onions needed a little longer. Marcus Alcott placed the lid on the pot to let them simmer further before adding the chicken and other vegetables to the meal he was cooking for himself and his seventy-one-year-old mother, Ruth. The tantalising aroma of the onions made his stomach rumble, but he was a patient man, and he'd wait until they were cooked to perfection.

He turned as his mother wheeled herself into the kitchen. Bending down, Marcus kissed her soft cheek. "Hello, Mum. How was your study?" Ruth suffered from severe arthritis, but it didn't stop her from attending her weekly Bible study group.

"Wonderful as always, dear," she replied in her sweet voice. "Something smells nice. What are you cooking?"

"Your favourite. Stir-fried chicken and vegetables."

"You do spoil me, Marcus." His mother's eyes twinkled as she wheeled closer. "What can I do to help?"

"It's all in hand, Mum. Just relax."

"Okay. Thank you, love." She shifted back, giving him space. A few moments later she asked, "Do you remember Stacie Templeton?"

Marcus ran a hand through his thick, brown hair. His mum knew so many people, but he thought he remembered her. "I think so."

"Well, she mentioned that her daughter's company is catering for the annual Breast Cancer Fundraising Ball this year."

Marcus stiffened as a shudder raced up his spine. He knew what was coming next.

"Have you decided who you're taking?" His mother quirked a brow.

Trying to appear distracted, he quickly turned to the pot and lifted the lid and inspected the onions again.

"Marcus?"

He blew out a breath. "No, Mum. Not yet." Tipping the diced chicken into the pan, he grabbed a spatula and combined the chicken with the browned onions. "I'm working on it."

"Good. Make sure you do. I'll set the table."

As his mother disappeared into the adjoining dining room of the harbour-side mansion they shared, a relieved sigh escaped his lips. Why would any woman want to accompany him to a ball honouring his late wife? Bree, his childhood sweetheart and the love of his life, had succumbed to the insidious disease five years earlier. He was now the main patron of the fundraising event, an event which always revived memories of his beautiful wife who'd been taken too soon. He went through this same dilemma every year. Who would he invite?

Despite the memories it invoked, he loved the ball. The money raised funded research so other men needn't suffer the devastating loss he had. If only he could go on his own, but he was expected to take a partner—attending a ball on one's own was frowned upon in his social circle. He blew out another breath. He'd have to think who to invite soon, otherwise his mum would choose for him, and that could be disastrous.

His mother only wanted him to be happy again. He knew that. And although he didn't want to be alone for the rest of his life, he couldn't imagine marrying again, even though it was something his mother so clearly wanted. The very idea was painful and seemed unreasonable, even impossible.

They both knew what it was like to lose a spouse. Bree had succumbed to cancer, and his father had been killed by a teen drunk driver. Losing a spouse was an ache no one ever truly recovered from, but Ruth Alcott had done her best over the past ten years to live her life to the fullest, despite her loss and ailing health. She had no desire to marry again, but it didn't stop her from wishing Marcus would.

"Shall I add some peri-peri to the chicken?" he called out.

"Not tonight, dear. My stomach's a little sensitive today," his mum replied. Marcus grinned. It was the same answer she always gave. He'd add the spice separately to his own meal, like he always did.

As he continued cooking, memories of that day ten years earlier crossed his mind. He'd been at work when the call came from the police, and he'd rushed home to find his mum a

3

weeping mess. An eighteen-year-old woman had been arrested, but his dad was dead. He'd died instantly, and to begin with, neither Marcus nor his mum could believe it. The woman, Sally Hubbard, was sentenced and spent three years in jail for dangerous driving causing death. During that time, Marcus and Ruth came to forgive the young woman who displayed deep remorse over her actions but seemed a little unstable. They'd heard she'd spent some time in a Psychiatric Hospital undergoing treatment.

She still came around now and then to visit his mum. It was a strange relationship, and each time they saw her, memories were revived and their forgiveness tested. But as Christians, it was what they were called to do, so despite their sadness and loss, they forgave her and offered her kindness.

Marcus exhaled a deep sigh as he scooped the stir fry onto two plates and turned the gas off. This wasn't the life he'd imagined he'd be living right now. He and Bree had hoped for at least two children, but that had never eventuated. He didn't regret living with his mother—they provided companionship for each other, but sometimes he felt saddened by what might have been.

He carried the plates into the dining room, placing them onto the table before helping his mum into her ergonomic dining chair. He then filled two glasses with sparkling water and a squirt of lime juice.

"This looks lovely, dear." She smiled sweetly at him.

"Thanks, Mum." Returning her smile, Marcus took her hand and prayed over the meal, thanking God for all their blessings as well as the food before them. Despite having more money than he could ever need or use, he was very conscious that everything he had came from the Lord, and besides, after a busy day at work, it was always good to pause for a moment and settle his thoughts.

Letting go of his mother's hand, he sipped his water before adding some spiced seasoning to his meal. He'd just taken his first mouthful when she waved her fork in the air. She was mulling something over, and he knew what it was.

"I've been thinking a lot about the charity ball," she said, toying with her food.

His mother was far from manipulative, but she was an expert at getting him to listen even when he didn't want to. It had been a long day, and although his I.T. company practically ran itself, he still invested much time ensuring it continued to move forward. That involved detailed planning and long-winded meetings. Sensing his day was far from over, he took a deep breath and waited to hear what it was that she might have to say.

"What have you been thinking, Mum?"

"That you ought to invite Tiffany."

He blinked. "Tiffany?"

"Yes. She's a lovely young woman, and it would do her good to go out and enjoy herself. She's such a hard worker. And she's also quite beautiful," his mother added, her eyes twinkling.

Marcus inhaled deeply. He'd never thought of his mother's part-time caregiver as someone he might invite to an important event like the gala charity ball. Nothing against the woman; he'd just never considered her in that way. He did have to agree with his mother, though. Tiffany was attractive. But she was their employee. How could he invite her to the ball? No matter that she was an excellent caregiver to his mother, Tiffany was still…an employee. And he knew very little about her. Not that taking her would mean it was a date. But what if she considered it as such and it caused confusion in the future? Wasn't that why he hadn't invited any of the women from church? Because he didn't want them to get the wrong idea?

"I don't know about that, Mum. Don't you think it would be confusing? I mean, we hired her to do a job. If she's suddenly asked by her employer to be his date for the night, don't you think she might feel manipulated? Or that she'd get the wrong idea?"

"Oh, come now, Marcus. She'd understand. You can tell her she's doing you a favour, and I'm sure she'd be a wonderful companion for the evening."

He wasn't sure. Maybe he could ask her. Ensure she understood it was just for one evening. Like she was working. But still, it didn't entirely make sense that this was a good idea. It could cause problems. And even if it didn't, did he want to go to an event honouring his late wife with his mother's caregiver?

"I'll consider it," he promised. But as he ate his meal, he concluded that the idea was next to impossible. It simply wouldn't work.

CHAPTER 2

"Can you get the paperwork on my desk by Tuesday?" Marcus asked into the phone, leaning back in his chair.

His lawyer confirmed he could, and Marcus thanked the man before hanging up.

The new contract was about to settle, and he was excited. Pumped. It was the biggest contract since his company, Quantum Technology, had landed the deal with the Great Vacations Travel Company six years earlier. That contract had exponentially escalated the growth of his firm and taken it to where it was now—a Top Ten publicly listed company worth billions, and this new contract would keep it there.

It had been a risk when he and Bree bought the firm from his former boss, John O'Malley. They'd used their life savings to buy him out and lived on next to nothing while they built it up. Although they'd seen potential, they'd never expected it to be quite so successful. If only she was here to see the full fruit of their efforts.

Needing another coffee, Marcus pushed back in his chair and headed to the break room, smiling at employees he passed on the way. He had a great team, and he was glad for each and every one of them.

"Hi, Mr. Alcott," greeted Joan, the young barista who maintained the coffee and pastries for the staff.

"Hey, Joan," he replied in a friendly manner.

"Single or double?" she asked, knowing his order and its variations.

"I'm going to need a double today." He laughed lightly as he leaned against the counter.

"Easy enough!" She smiled before proceeding to make his americano.

After she finished, Marcus thanked her and strolled back to his office, sipping his coffee as he walked. Reaching his office, he noticed through the floor to ceiling glass wall that someone was sitting in the chair opposite his. Curious, he quickened his pace.

"Hello?" he said, entering his office. Typically, no one was allowed inside without his consent, although he never locked his door.

The slim young woman stood slowly and turned to him. He stopped mid-stride, his mouth dropping open.

"Marcus!" she greeted, stepping to him and giving him a firm hug.

Marcus stiffened. "S-Sally." He tried to pry himself from her grip. The way she greeted him with such familiarity was strange. Unusual. He'd never known her to do that, and he was quite sure he didn't want her to do it again.

Once she released him, he gestured for her to sit. As she did, she pushed her large, thick-rimmed glasses up her nose and smiled as if they were best friends.

"What are you doing here?" he asked, as he walked around the large mahogany desk and eased into his director's chair.

"I thought I'd stop by and say hello since I've just started working somewhere pretty special." Her voice had taken on a sing-song tone, like she wanted him to guess where it was she worked. He didn't have time to play games, but he also didn't want to be rude. "And where's that, Sally?"

"Great Vacations!" she exclaimed, her heavily dyed black bob bouncing as she sat tall, her eyes wide.

"That's great, Sally. I'm really happy for you." He knew she hadn't worked much since getting out of jail, and that any job she'd had had been in the service industry or in a retail store. Getting a position with a company like Great Vacations was a huge achievement, and he was glad for her.

"Thanks! Honestly, I'd never thought about working in travel, but when I heard that they were working with your firm, I thought it was a great fit," she said with a nervous laugh.

Marcus's brows furrowed. He wasn't sure how to interpret her statement, but he nodded politely.

"So, I was also thinking about something else," Sally continued.

"Oh?" he replied. "And what's that?" He glanced at his computer screen as an alert popped up. He didn't have time to be sitting here chatting with Sally, but she seemed oblivious to the fact that he was a busy man and she hadn't made an appointment.

"Well, I know the charity ball is coming up soon. I mean, I just thought you should know that I'd love to go with you. I know it's a difficult time for you, and I'd be honoured to be by your side on such a challenging evening." She spoke with such compassion that he was completely taken aback. *The charity ball? She's offering to go to the charity ball with me?* He ran his hand across his hair. It was thoughtful of her to acknowledge the evening would be challenging for him, but the thought of taking her was far stranger than the thought of taking Tiffany.

"Wow, Sally, that's so nice of you to think of me and to have that sort of empathy. I really appreciate it," Marcus said diplomatically. "I'll keep it in mind, but I do have a friend I'm planning to take this year."

Sally's smile faltered slightly, but she kept her spirits up and Marcus was glad she didn't seem offended. "Oh, great! I didn't know you were already making plans with someone. I was just thinking about it and figured if you didn't have a date yet, I'd let you know that I'm free that night."

Marcus smiled at her. It was kind of her to be so thoughtful. His mother didn't think Sally had fully recovered from the trauma of the accident, even after ten years, and that she still felt guilt over the loss of his father. To know she was trying to take steps to look out for others was definitely a positive sign.

"I really am appreciative, Sally. I'll let you know if my plans change," he said, leaving it at that.

Standing, Sally smiled and slipped on her black jacket. "For sure! Anyway, I hope you have a great rest of the day," she remarked, shaking Marcus's hand by way of farewell.

After she was gone, Marcus thought through the exchange. It was clear that Sally still struggled to interact with people, that she was oblivious of social cues, but she seemed to be making an attempt. That was the good part. But it also confirmed to him that he needed to make a decision. He'd told her he was taking a friend to the ball, so now he had no option but to invite Tiffany. As an employee, she'd understand better than any of his other female friends that it was a date of convenience and that nothing more would be expected of her. It wasn't ideal, but he couldn't risk not having a date with Sally circling.

CHAPTER 3

"*And* I…just can't say…goodbye," Tiffany Harris belted out, holding onto the last note as she pulled into the back entrance of the Alcott estate. She turned off the engine but sat in the car until the song finished on the radio.

Gazing out over the back of the estate, she wondered why anyone would need a tennis court. It seemed an extravagance, but the pool, now that was something she'd love to have in her backyard. Her kids would absolutely love one, but it would have to be much smaller. The Alcott's pool was so huge it'd never fit in her pocket-sized yard.

Wednesdays were Ruth days. Tiffany loved Ruth days. Her other client, Mrs. Honeycutt, was a far less pleasant woman to be around, but still, Tiffany loved her job. With Ruth Alcott, she was able to relax and be herself. She oftentimes felt more like a friend than a caregiver to the elderly woman.

Ruth had terrible arthritis and was wheelchair bound, but

that was easy for Tiffany. Ruth still had her wits about her, and she was feisty and interesting.

Reaching the back door, Tiffany knocked and called for Ruth, enjoying the warmth of the sun on her back while she waited to be called in. Instead of hearing her client's voice, Tiffany was surprised to see Ruth's son approach the door.

"Oh, Mr. Alcott, how are you?" she asked with a warm smile. Although he'd always been friendly in their brief interactions, they'd never spoken much so she didn't know him as well as she knew his mother.

"Tiffany...hi," he replied, holding the door open for her. "Mum's in her craft room, looking for some buttons to take to one of the ladies at her Bible study."

"No problem. I can wait here for her. We still have time before we need to head out," Tiffany said. Wednesday mornings she took Ruth to her Bible study group.

"So, I actually wanted to talk to you about something," he said slowly, rubbing the back of his neck.

Tiffany's heart began to pound. Was he about to let her go? Had she done something wrong? She couldn't afford to lose the job.

"I know this probably seems strange, but do you know anything about the Breast Cancer Charity Ball?" he asked.

She'd heard of it, but she couldn't imagine why he was bringing it up. "I think so. I mean, it's a pretty big event, right?"

"Yes..." he replied, his voice trailing off.

Tiffany wondered at his anxiety when he always seemed so confident.

"So, anyway, I'm expected to take a date." He paused and slowly lifted his gaze to hers, swallowing visibly. "I know this might sound a bit strange since we don't know one another well, but my mother suggested I invite you this year."

Tiffany's eyes widened. Never in her wildest dreams had she expected an invitation to a ball from a man like Marcus Alcott. Confused, she wasn't sure how she felt about it. Inviting her was clearly a matter of convenience, but even so, she would never have expected him to invite her. She was just an employee, after all.

Although she'd been caught off-guard, she maintained eye contact with her boss, looking into his deep brown eyes with astonishment. "Wow..." she finally managed to say. "I wasn't expecting that."

"Yeah." He laughed nervously. "I know it seems a bit strange, but Mum thought you might enjoy it. If you don't want to go, I'll understand, but I'd be happy if you'd agree to come with me."

The shock hadn't fully worn off, but Tiffany tried to look at the situation rationally. He was a good man. Of course, she thought she'd found such a man once before, but Steve had been anything but good.

Presumably, Marcus Alcott was only asking her to be his date because he couldn't find another, although she would have assumed any number of women would be more than willing to accompany him. It wasn't as though he was trying to start a relationship with her, but it still made her wonder what it would be like to go on a date with him. Especially to such a prestigious event.

She'd never been to an event like the ball before. She had nothing to wear and couldn't afford to buy anything or even get fabric for her mum to make her something. Not to mention the fact that she couldn't assume her parents would mind the kids. It was simply too complicated.

"I'd really love to go with you, but I don't know if I can find anything to wear or a sitter for my kids," she said, listing the two reasons that would prevent her from going. But would those reasons be enough to avoid offending the Alcotts if she decided to decline his invitation? The last thing she wanted was to hurt his feelings or create miscommunication. *Or lose her job.*

"I can arrange everything. Honestly, you don't have to worry about a thing." He seemed to be almost pleading with her, which puzzled Tiffany. Why would a man like Marcus Alcott, a stunningly handsome billionaire, have trouble finding a date for an event like this? *Why would he even ask her?*

Although the invitation was flattering and she had no reason to distrust him, after everything she'd been through with Steve, she was off men altogether. If she went, and it was a big 'if', she'd sort the details herself. She wasn't going to be dependent on anyone. Not even a billionaire. Who knew what he might want of her next? But she didn't want to be rude. "I'll think about it and see if I can get things arranged on my end," she told him.

"Good. But I'd like to help if I can. Let me know? Oh, and by the way, please call me Marcus."

She nodded, excused herself, and went to find Ruth. On the way, she stopped in a darkened alcove, leaned against the wall, and took several deep breaths. Had that just happened? Had Marcus Alcott just invited her to a ball? She could hardly believe it.

After regaining her composure, Tiffany continued through

the house and found Ruth in her bedroom. It was hard concentrating when her mind was filled with balls and billionaires, but she was determined not to say anything to her employer. Since Ruth had been the instigator, however, Tiffany sensed she knew her son might have spoken to her, especially since she winked and grinned when Tiffany entered the room.

Later that day, after finishing her time with Ruth, Tiffany went to visit her parents and pick up her children. Mike and Polly were upstairs playing, so Tiffany had some time to sit with her mum and chat awhile.

"I like your haircut," her mum, Marjorie, complimented.

"Thanks!" Tiffany gave her hair a little flick. She'd needed a change, and now her dark brown hair sat just above her shoulders instead of below. She wasn't sure if she liked it or not, but a change was as good as a holiday. Although sometimes she thought a real holiday would have to be better.

"So, what's got you so distracted?" her mum asked.

"What do you mean?" Tiffany frowned.

"You're my daughter, and I can tell you've got something on your mind."

Tiffany let out a small chuckle. There was no fooling her mum. As she recounted the whole story, she felt even more confused than she had earlier in the day when Marcus invited her to the ball. Every time she replayed the conversation in her mind, her amazement did not dwindle.

"Are you serious?" her mum asked with a spark in her eyes.

"Yes…" Tiffany replied hesitantly.

"You have to accept, Tiffany. And don't worry about the dress. I'll take care of that," her mother insisted.

"Mum, I can't ask—"

"Let me spoil my little girl for once. We'll get you looking like a million dollars. No doubt about it. You can't use lame excuses to avoid something as special as this," she continued.

Still not entirely convinced it was a good idea, Tiffany drew a deep breath. Going to the ball with her employer seemed like such a crazy thing to do. But if her mum was so insistent, maybe she should consider it.

"Before I forget, can the kids come with us to church on Sunday?" her mum asked out of the blue.

Tiffany pursed her lips. "You took them last week."

"And they really enjoyed it." Her mum lifted a brow.

Tiffany pondered. She knew her kids loved going to church with their grandparents and that the Sunday school classes were fun for them, but she wasn't entirely comfortable with them going. She honestly didn't see the point. But they'd be disappointed if they didn't go. She let out a resigned sigh. "Alright, I guess they can go."

When her mother smiled and gave her hand a squeeze, Tiffany hid a grimace. She knew her mum would like her to go as well, but Tiffany had grown skeptical of church and religion and saw no reason to go.

CHAPTER 4

*a*rriving in the office on Thursday morning, Marcus saw the light flashing on his desk phone. He figured it was probably another client updating him on things, but when he checked the voicemail, he was completely caught off guard again.

"Hey Mark, it's me, Sally. Of course. Anyway, I hope you're doing well. I just wanted to give you a call to see where you're at with things as far as the charity ball is concerned. I'm really glad you're considering me for the date, but I thought I'd see if there was an update.

"Sorry, maybe I should have come to see you in person so we could talk more about all of this. But anyway, I figured I'd call first. I'm just so glad for your kindness and everything. I mean, you're so successful and strong and really amazing. I'm glad to be working so closely with you. Like we're business partners or something.

"But anyway, I know that we'll see a lot more of each other now that we're working so close together. Thanks, Mark. Really. Just give me a call whenever you've decided what you're doing about the ball."

With that, the message ended.

Marcus leaned back in his chair. From the very beginning of the message he'd been distracted. Since when did Sally think it was okay to call him Mark? Did she not know that he went by Marcus, or did she think she was being familiar by shortening his name?

The message unnerved him. It was fine that Sally was enthusiastic about her new position, but she seemed to be spending a lot of time thinking about him. He tried not to be annoyed. She was a young woman in need of a friend. And help. She definitely needed help.

Even after ten years and a short stay in a Psychiatric Hospital after her release from jail, she was still clearly overwhelmed by what she'd done, and perhaps being overly friendly with him was her attempt to get over it, but Marcus didn't know how much more he could reasonably handle. She needed to deal with her guilt in a more appropriate way. She couldn't work herself into his life in order to forgive herself.

There were plenty of places she could go to for help, and although he and his mum had given her suggestions, she'd never shown any enthusiasm about seeking out psychological or faith-based counseling. Sighing, he sent up a quick prayer for her and deleted the message.

A short while later, Marcus made his way to a meeting and then dealt with a few issues that needed attention. The company was doing well financially, but there was still a great deal of day-to-day pressure.

Arriving home, he found his mother on the back deck, looking out over the harbour. "Hey Mum, how was your day?" he asked, giving her a peck on the cheek.

"Good. But Thursdays are my boring day," she reminded him.

"I know. But did you at least get some reading done?" he asked.

"Of course. That's about all there is for me to do on Tuesdays and Thursdays. I wish Tiffany could come every day," she said wistfully.

"She'll be here tomorrow." He gave her a smile and poured himself an orange juice from the outdoor bar before sitting beside her.

Tiffany still hadn't gotten back to him about whether or not she would be his date for the ball. Should he take her silence as a no? Or did she just need more time? No doubt his invitation had thrown her.

"Yes. She's such a lovely girl."

Marcus knew where she was leading but didn't take the bait. "I'll get started on dinner," he said, standing. He went into the kitchen to begin cooking, but Bree's photo on the kitchen dresser caught his attention. He walked over and picked it up. She'd loved this house, and especially this kitchen with its European appliances and Italian marble counter-tops. How he wished she were still alive. He'd give everything he had to have her back.

The only thing he could do was donate money to the charity to ensure that no other man had to lose his wife to such a vicious disease. He didn't want anyone else to hurt the way he was hurting. It wasn't fair that he'd lost Bree, and it wouldn't be fair to any other husbands or fathers or children to lose the women in their lives to something so dreadful. But it happened. It happened all the time. And for that reason, he had to keep moving forward and do all he could to prevent it.

But the thought of taking a date to the ball still filled him with anxiety. If Tiffany rejected him, would he take Sally? He let out a huge sigh. No, she wasn't an option. If Tiffany said no, he'd have to find someone else or go alone. The last thing he wanted was to become Sally's only source of therapy. She needed professional help and that was something he couldn't give her.

"You didn't tell me how work was," his mum said, wheeling into the kitchen.

He pushed thoughts of the ball aside. "It was fine. Lots of meetings, but things are going really well. We're closing with a new client tomorrow—another huge contract. The one I told you about last month."

"I knew you'd get it," his mum replied with pride in her voice.

"The team worked really hard and I'm proud of them. I couldn't have gotten this far if they hadn't done so much to make it all come to pass," he said humbly.

His mother was watching him, but he went about his cooking, trying to stay busy. He felt like she was observing him the way a scientist eyed a specimen. She was a concerned mother and he could understand that, but he didn't want her to always feel so concerned about him.

"What is it?" he asked with a gentle smile.

"Your father would be really proud of you, Marcus."

It wasn't what he'd been expecting, but his heart warmed at knowing his mother was proud of him and his father would have been, too.

CHAPTER 5

*T*iffany couldn't sleep. Marcus's invitation to the charity ball had been consuming her thoughts for nearly two whole days. She'd most likely be seeing him again on Friday morning and would have to give her answer. An answer she still hadn't made up her mind about.

On one hand, she was tempted to go. The thought of getting dressed up and accompanying a handsome, wealthy man to a ball was certainly appealing. Not to mention the fact that her mother had been urging her to accept.

But how could she go? She'd never been to anything close to a ball in her life and she wouldn't have the first clue about how to act. And Marcus Alcott was far from the sort of man she could ever be involved with, so it wasn't as though she could even consider that.

Yes, it would be foolish to pretend to be his date.

These thoughts swirled round and round in her head all night. At 2.43 a.m. she glanced once more at her clock before she finally fell into a disturbed sleep. When her alarm went off at 6:00 a.m., she was completely exhausted and didn't want to get out of bed. Nevertheless, she had to get the kids ready for school and ready herself for work.

Once they were out the door and she'd dropped the kids at school, she headed to the office of The Angels of Care to do some paperwork before making her way to the Alcott estate.

During the entire drive she felt anxious, the pressure of the charity ball gnawing at her gut. What would she say to Marcus? What if he asked her again and she still didn't have an answer? And why didn't she have an answer? She should just say no.

She drove her car into the parking space and went inside, calling for Ruth. Looking around, Tiffany was prepared for an encounter with Marcus, but to her enormous relief, he didn't seem to be present.

"Hello, dear," Ruth greeted, wheeling her chair into the kitchen.

Tiffany smiled at her favourite client. "Have you had breakfast already? I can smell bacon."

"Yes, Marcus had an early morning meeting but made breakfast before he left. There's some left if you're hungry," Ruth offered.

"Thank you, but I'm good. I ate at home." Tiffany sighed with relief. Marcus wasn't there. She wouldn't have to give him an answer yet.

"Alright then, dear. Can you help me get dressed?"

"Sure." Tiffany smiled and pushed Ruth's wheelchair through the sprawling mansion to her bedroom and helped her dress. Ruth struggled to perform such simple tasks, but she always tried to do things herself. Although not totally incapacitated, walking caused her such great pain that she only walked when she had to. Tiffany felt such respect for the elderly woman who never complained, unlike Mrs. Honeycutt.

"What's the plan for today?" Tiffany asked brightly after helping Ruth into a warm pair of trousers and a matching twinset. Fridays were never a consistent schedule and Ruth often surprised her.

"I thought we could go for a walk this morning and then, this afternoon, there's a women's event at church I'd love to go to."

Tiffany nodded with a smile. On the days Ruth went to church events and Bible study, she mostly sat in the car reading while she waited for Ruth to finish. She enjoyed those days since they gave her an opportunity for peaceful downtime she typically didn't get being a single mum of two. Mike and Polly were great kids, but looking after them on her own was tiring, so she snatched whatever respite she could.

Soon, they made their way out the front door to the path that weaved around the estate. It was a glorious morning with a slight freshness in the air. "Are you sure you don't want to go to the park?" Tiffany asked.

"No, I'm happy to stay here today."

"That's okay. I thought you might like to go somewhere different, that's all."

"Speaking of going somewhere different..." Ruth lifted an eyebrow.

Tiffany groaned. She'd said the wrong thing. Of course, Ruth was going to home in on that topic now. Why hadn't she been more cautious with her words? "Yes?" she asked hesitantly.

"You seem a little jumpy today. Is there something on your mind? You appear distracted," Ruth said, angling her head.

Tiffany bit her lip. She couldn't lie. "Maybe a little," she replied honestly.

"Is it anything to do with Marcus? Did he, by any chance, invite you to an event?"

Tiffany blew out a breath. There was no point denying it. "Yes, yes he did," she answered.

"Oh, how wonderful! I was hoping he'd asked you. Have you made up your mind to go?"

This was awkward. Tiffany didn't want to insult Ruth by refusing her son. But she also didn't want to lie. She hadn't made up her mind yet, and that was the truth, but the thought of accepting the invitation and all that it entailed filled her with anxiety. "There's a lot I have to consider first. I'd need to find someone to mind my kids. That's my first priority," she said, again hoping she could lay all the blame on being a single mother so she wouldn't offend the Alcotts if she refused Marcus's invitation, although she knew it wasn't really a valid excuse. Her mum had already offered to mind the kids and to help with the dress.

"Absolutely. They must always remain your top priority, but you do need to think of yourself as well, dear. I think you should go. It won't be an easy evening for Marcus, and I'm sure you'd be good company for him."

Tiffany didn't know much about Marcus's wife, but she knew enough to understand why it would be a challenging event for him. She also guessed it might be hard for him to take a date when it was an event honouring his late wife. She could hardly blame him for struggling to find somebody to go with.

"I suppose it wouldn't do any harm...so long as my parents can mind Mike and Polly," Tiffany finally said. She'd allow herself a small indulgence. Just once. And she'd face her anxiety head on. She could do this. If not for herself, for Marcus.

Ruth smiled. "Marcus doesn't enjoy being in the spotlight. He avoids it as much as he can, but he goes because he has to, and because it's for such a worthy cause. He won't leave you on your own—he'll look after you the whole evening."

Tiffany had no doubt Ruth was right, although she didn't really go for the chivalrous types. She was too independent for that. Nevertheless, if she could make Marcus's evening a little easier, maybe she could agree to be his date.

CHAPTER 6

"And how are things going with the new contract?" Ruth asked Marcus on Sunday morning as they drove towards their church.

"Great. I felt bad making Hodge come in yesterday so he could file the papers. I don't like making the guys work on Saturdays. I rarely have to, and it doesn't seem right making them do it," Marcus replied.

The contract had been finalised and he was confident that this newest venture would take the business to another level altogether. They'd been doing so well since obtaining the Great Vacations contract, but winning the deal with Money Solutions was something else, and he was thrilled about it. Bree would have been so proud.

"You really do pour yourself into your work," his mum commented.

"It's a big part of my life," he agreed.

"Yes, but don't let it be the only part of your life." She raised a brow.

"It's not, you know that. I also have you. And you're way more important to me than work will ever be," he said, glancing from the road to her.

She grinned back at him, but it was clear she wasn't finished with what she wanted to say. "Now Marcus, I'm glad you're doing so well these days, but when I talk about you pouring yourself into work, or spending so much time with your doddering old mum—"

"You're hardly doddering," he interjected.

"Well, either way, it's important that you don't neglect yourself. You should make efforts to do what you want now and then."

"I think I do."

"I disagree. I hardly see you doing anything for yourself. You know that's why I'm urging you to take someone to the ball. You need to go out and enjoy yourself once in a while."

Marcus quietly nodded. She was right. He knew she was right, but he didn't necessarily want to listen or admit it. His loneliness was more evident to his mother than anyone. Even his sister hardly bothered him about these things. It was understandable. She had her own life to live, a family to care for.

They reached the church and Marcus helped his mum out of the vehicle. He pushed her along the path to the entrance where they were greeted warmly by the friendly elders. They entered the chapel and Marcus positioned his mum's wheelchair into the space especially set aside for her towards the front before he sat on the pew next to her.

"Just think about it, that's all." His mum patted his hand. "You deserve happiness, Marcus," she said once more as the worship band made their way to the front of the church and the service began.

He tried to shut out his personal concerns and focus on worshiping God throughout the songs and hymns that followed.

When the worship time ended, the pastor, an older man who was well respected amongst his parishioners, stood behind the pulpit. He began by praying and asking God to bless the message before reading a passage of Scripture from Isaiah twenty-eight.

"Have you not known? Have you not heard? The Lord is the everlasting God, the Creator of the ends of the earth. He does not faint or grow weary; His understanding is unsearchable. He gives power to the faint, and to him who has no might he increases strength. Even youths shall faint and be weary, and young men shall fall exhausted; but they who wait for the Lord shall renew their strength; they shall mount up with wings like eagles; they shall run and not be weary; they shall walk and not faint.

"I love this passage as it reminds me that our Lord is so much greater than I can ever think or imagine. He is the everlasting God, the Creator of heaven and earth, and is worthy of our praise. Despite His greatness and majesty, He cares for each and every one of us. We might find that difficult to comprehend when we face challenges, but He gives those who love Him strength to face them, and He promises that all those who wait upon Him shall mount up like eagles. Take heart if you're struggling today and call upon the name of the Lord. He might not remove your challenges, but He will give you strength to face them."

Marcus had struggled to believe that God truly cared when Bree died. He'd always believed that God was good and that He had a plan and a purpose for his and Bree's life, but after she passed, he struggled to find the good in her death and began to question God. It took a lot of soul searching and praying, but finally, he'd accepted that God's ways were higher than his. Once he'd accepted that, he'd found peace.

Although Bree was now with God and no longer had any suffering or pain, he was still alone and missed her terribly. Sometimes he still questioned God before he realised he had no right to.

Church ended and they chatted with some other worshippers for a short while. He'd promised to take his mum to her favourite restaurant for lunch, so he wheeled her back to the car and then headed into the city.

After reaching the restaurant at Double Bay, they placed their orders and chatted for a while about the church service.

"On another topic, I got a strange phone call yesterday," his mother said while removing her glasses.

"Oh? From whom?" Marcus asked.

"Sally. She was asking about you. Have you seen her lately?"

He sighed. "Yes, I should have told you, but I've had a lot of things going on and I forgot. She's started working at Great Vacations and I've seen her at work once. She left a voicemail on my phone on Thursday." He then told her about Sally inviting herself to the ball.

"Hmm," she said, frowning. "I don't like her bothering you like that, and she shouldn't be inviting herself to the ball."

"Neither do I. I don't know what she's trying to do, but she still seems a little unstable."

"We ought to pray for her."

"That's a good idea. She really needs help."

"I've tried to help her. Believe me."

"I know you have, Mum. You've been more than patient with her. More than she deserves."

"We're called to be kind, Marcus. You know that, but I'm not sure how much more we can do for her."

"Like you said, we can pray for her. We'll pray that she finds peace and that she can forgive herself."

"Yes. I think that's all we can do."

Their meals arrived, and Marcus included Sally in his prayer of thanks before they ate.

CHAPTER 7

*A*rriving at the Alcott estate on Monday morning, Tiffany had finally made up her mind. She knew exactly what she would do and what she would say when she saw Marcus Alcott. She had no other choice.

Still, the moment she actually laid eyes on him in the kitchen where he stood, facing away from her, she was distracted by the broadness of his shoulders and his tall, well-proportioned body. Her reaction surprised her.

She shook it off, embarrassed that her resolve to treat the ball as nothing more than an extension of her job had almost been derailed by his physical appearance. After all, it wouldn't work if she started to think of Marcus as anything other than her client's son. Her employer. And as she'd vowed never to marry again, there was no reason to allow herself to even look at him in that way.

"Good morning," she said, knocking at the open door and poking her head in.

He turned and faced her.

"Oh, hello. Good morning," he greeted. He was putting away some sort of powder that he'd added to a smoothie. No wonder he looked healthy if he was consuming that stuff. Tiffany had seen it at the store and remembered how expensive it was.

"Sorry, am I early?" she asked. The house was abnormally silent.

"Mum isn't awake yet, but you're right on time. She was exhausted after yesterday. I should have called to give you a heads up so you didn't rush over."

"Don't worry, I had to drop my kids at school, anyway," she replied. "And I did want to talk to you." Tiffany felt her heart beating a little faster thanks to the commitment she was about to make. Going to a charity ball with a man like Marcus Alcott was not something to take lightly. But she had to press on and tell him what she was thinking.

"Oh?"

"Yes. About the charity ball." She swallowed hard. "I think I've got everything sorted. My parents can mind the kids, so if the invitation is still open, I'd like to accept."

"That's wonderful! I'm glad you got it worked out. And don't worry, I'll take care of everything else. My sister can go shopping with you. And I'll pay for your dress."

"Whoa. Hang on a minute. I'll get all of that sorted myself, thank you," she replied tersely. She wasn't about to be taken over, not even by a good-looking billionaire.

His expression fell. "Oh, of course you can. I'm really sorry, I wasn't thinking," he said quickly.

She gave him a muted smile. She'd have to rely on her mum

for the dress, and maybe her sister for hair and makeup. No way would she allow herself to be bought or considered a charity case. She was independent and proud, and she needed him to see that. "Well, I'll look forward to the ball. Thank you for inviting me."

"It's my pleasure, and I'm looking forward to taking you." His smile almost derailed her again. She quickly took hold of herself while he went about preparing to leave for work. She remained downstairs until Ruth was up and about, then went to help her get dressed. The two of them headed out to visit some of Ruth's friends and to get groceries.

After that, Tiffany drove to her mum's home to talk over everything she would need in preparation for the ball.

"I don't know what to wear, Mum. I could go to a charity shop, but the people who'll be at the ball are the sort who send their clothes to those shops. What if I buy a dress one of them wore two years ago?"

"I told you I'd make your dress," her mum reminded her.

"I know, but I don't have money for fabric."

"Then I guess it's a good thing navy suits you, because I've got plenty of it." Her mother grinned.

"Navy? That could work. What kind of fabric is it?"

"Exactly the kind you'd want for a fancy charity ball."

"It's a black-tie affair so I'll have to wear a long dress. Is there enough fabric?"

"Yes. It was a cancelled order. Let me grab it," her mum said, leaving Tiffany alone for a moment.

When she returned, Tiffany's breath caught. The fabric was beautiful. Rich in colour but soft to the touch.

"And this lace goes with it."

"This is incredible, Mum. I love it. Thank you so much." Wrapping her arms around her mother, she gave her a big hug as excitement about the ball grew within her. She could check out some charity shops for shoes and jewelry. She wouldn't need much, maybe some paste diamonds for earrings, a pair of heels, and a small purse.

She might grow anxious again, but right now, she couldn't help the small tremor of anticipation that flowed through her. She was going to a ball with a billionaire! *How had that happened?*

"Thank you for everything, Mum." She gave her mother another hug.

"Anything for my little girl." Her mum smiled. Tiffany thought she saw tears in her eyes.

CHAPTER 8

"*A*re you sure we didn't need to bring anything more than this?" Ruth asked, holding up one of the breadsticks she'd bought at the local bakery.

Marcus glanced at his mum but continued driving with a grin on his face. "It's more than enough. Ebony said they have everything in hand. There's no need to worry."

"I suppose you're right. She always makes more than enough."

"Yes, she does." It was actually an understatement—his sister always over catered. In fact, she could almost feed an entire family for a week with what she prepared whenever he and his mum visited. It was as if she were trying to over-compensate for not having as much money as he did. He'd lost count how many times he'd assured her she had nothing to prove, but he understood how she must feel when she and Jason lived week to week, and he had more money than he knew what to do with. They wouldn't accept help. He could understand that they had pride, but he would have gladly helped them out and not thought any less of them, but they were proud people and always refused his offer.

Arriving after the hour-long drive, Marcus climbed out of the car and stretched. His nine-year-old nephew, Harry, ran out the door to greet them and almost knocked him over. Marcus lifted his nephew in his arms and groaned under the boy's weight as he swung him around.

"You're getting so big!" he exclaimed. At five years of age, Ella and Lily were much easier to pick up. In fact, he often carried one in each arm.

Marcus loved seeing the kids, but he always felt a tinge of sadness as well. He and Bree had tried IVF after learning they couldn't conceive naturally, but it hadn't been successful. They'd agreed to consider adoption, but then Bree got sick.

Ebony and Jason invited Marcus and his mother inside. Jason took over the wheelchair and wheeled Ruth inside. The house was small and didn't have the ramps and railings to accommodate Ruth like his estate did. But it didn't matter—it was always a joy to visit.

They sat down to a meal of spaghetti, meatballs and bread, and there was plenty left over. Afterwards, the children went to play in another room while the adults chatted in the living room while drinking coffee and eating chocolate.

"Do you remember that time Dad accidentally took my prenatal pills thinking they were multivitamins?" Ebony reminisced, eliciting laughter from the others. It had been just a few months prior to his death, when Ebony was about four months pregnant with Harry.

It was still hard for Marcus to think that his dad never got to meet any of his grandchildren. They continued telling stories about him, remembering the good times and ignoring the bad. Not that there were many of the latter. His dad had been a wonderful husband and father, and he would have been a doting grandfather. Marcus said nothing about Sally, although thoughts of her recent strange behaviour flitted through his mind. But then the conversation shifted and they talked about how much their dad had loved Bree.

It saddened Marcus to think that two people he loved so much had both gone. It didn't get any easier as they all, including himself, shared stories about her and how much they all cared about her.

They didn't talk about her every time they got together, but when they did, despite the grief the conversation revived, in many ways, talking about her brought him much happiness. It was comforting to know that he wasn't the only one who missed her.

"Hey, how's John doing?" Jason asked, after a few moments of silence had passed.

Marcus smiled gratefully, aware that he'd changed the topic of conversation on purpose. "He's doing really well. Retired in Florida."

"Florida?"

"Yes, he has family in the States and decided to head there. After we bought Quantum Solutions, he started another small firm and sold that one as well. He's a great businessman, but he's better at buying and selling businesses than running them," Marcus said with a laugh.

He was still so thankful to the man who'd given him such a great start. John O'Malley was a brilliant man, but it was true that he didn't always know how to scale his businesses and take them to the next level. That was Marcus's forté. He had an entrepreneurial spirit and was glad he'd gotten the opportunity to build Quantum Solutions and make it what it was now.

"I heard about the newest contract. Congratulations, big brother," Ebony said with respect in her voice. Marcus thanked her, still feeling the glow of pride for what his firm had accomplished with the latest project. It was the coup of the year.

"You know, you're probably one of the richest men in Sydney," she added.

He nodded. It was true. In fact, he knew exactly which number he ranked. Not because he kept track of it, but because some of the local business magazines announced the rankings each year. "But money isn't everything. I'd trade it all to have Bree back."

Ebony nodded sadly. She knew how much he missed her.

Marcus and his family continued conversing, but the ache in his heart remained. Would it ever ease? Would he ever be able to talk about Bree without this heaviness weighing him down?

The thought of going to the ball with Tiffany felt like a betrayal to Bree. She still held his heart, even though she was no longer here.

When it came time to leave, there were hugs and kisses all round. They'd already said goodnight to the kids who were now in bed. It was always difficult to leave. Although Ebony and Jason were far from rich, they were rich in other ways, ways that were far more important. They had each other, and they were raising three beautiful children. These were things that money couldn't buy. It was sometimes difficult for Marcus to not be envious.

"Did you have a nice time?" his mother asked quietly after he pulled away from the house and his sleek BMW purred down the freeway.

"Of course. Did you?"

"I had a great time. I always do. They're such a lovely family. And I'm glad the breadsticks were enough," she said, chuckling.

Marcus gave her a smile and then focused on the road ahead, his thoughts still with Bree. *Lord, I miss her so much. You know that. Please help me to see the way forward.*

CHAPTER 9

*P*ulling into Steve's driveway always made Tiffany feel sick to her stomach. Anytime she had to see her ex-husband, it was too much. Anytime she had to think about him, it was too much. But since he was the father of her children, she tried to ignore her anxiety and anger and not speak ill of him in front of Polly and Mike. But inside, she always felt as if she were falling apart.

His house was nicer than hers. She didn't know how he could afford the trendy home in the fashionable suburb of Rose Bay when he wasn't even working. She held down a full-time job yet struggled to pay the rent on a two-bedroom duplex in Newtown. Not that it was a competition, but she wanted to prove that she could take care of the kids better than he could. Nevertheless, every time she saw his home, she felt bitter at the unfairness of it all.

The kids raced to see who could reach the door first, and this time, Mike won, meaning he got to ring the doorbell. Polly pouted because she lost, but when Steve opened the door, they were both full of smiles again.

Although Steve made very little effort to interact with the children, they both scrambled for his attention. Mike wanted to show what a strong boy he was, and Polly wanted to climb onto his lap for safety and protection. Things Tiffany believed every child should have.

Yet Steve offered neither.

He let the children into the house while Tiffany stood outside to speak with him on the porch.

Leaning against the door frame, his hair was scruffy as if he'd just woken up. He was also carrying more weight than the last time she'd seen him.

He was close enough for her to smell that he was sober, one of the rules of their visits. In truth, she was far more gracious with him than she needed to be. But he knew that if he was drunk when she arrived with the kids, she'd take them away immediately and he might never see them again.

For Steve, the visits weren't so much about spending time with the kids. They were just another method of control. A reminder to Tiffany that he still had rights over some parts of her life.

"I'll be back at four," she confirmed.

"Got it," he said, turning to go inside.

"That's not all."

Stopping, he turned to face her, rolling his eyes and sighing. This was how he played, this part of him that acted like a teenage boy who didn't want to listen to his mother. She rolled her eyes in reply to let him know she understood his game.

She drew a deep breath and braced herself for his reaction

to what she was about to ask of him. "I've been caring for the kids without asking you for anything, but that needs to change. Mike wants to play football at school this term, and the fees and uniform aren't cheap. You need to get a job and start paying child support," she said bluntly, not caring to sugarcoat the reality.

He scoffed. "Child support? You want that from me now? You've not needed it before, so why do you suddenly need it now?" He stood over her like he used to, but she held her ground.

"I just told you why. It's not for me, Steve. It's for your son. Your son who wants you to be proud of him and to see him as a strong young man. He wants to play sports and it's unfair because I can't afford it without your help. It's time you stepped up and fulfilled your role as their father." Tiffany's heart pounded, but she was determined to remain firm. The fear she used to feel when she stood up to him had been far worse when they were together. He knew that if he tried anything now, he would never see the kids again and he would have no more power over her.

But it didn't stop her from feeling sick. Standing firm in front of Steve had never been easy and would never be.

His lips twisted and he shifted closer. Close enough for her to see the broken capillaries on his face. Her stomach knotted, but she didn't flinch. A cruel smile twisted his face. "If you think having a job is so important, then why don't you go out and get a second one? You wanted full custody and I agreed. That means you cover the costs."

Her blood boiled, but she couldn't allow Steve to see that he'd upset her. She had to restrain herself and maintain control or he'd know he'd wounded her all over again, and she didn't want that. She pursed her lips. "Right. I suppose we always knew what you're worth. Nothing." The insult landed, but she was beyond relief when he clenched his fists in restraint instead of threat.

She didn't want him to grow angry since the kids would be with him the rest of the day, so she held her tongue. "I'll be back at four." Turning, she strode down the pathway to her car.

The door banged behind her and she could hear the kids laughing as he entered. They were excited to spend time with him. Tears welled in her eyes. It irked her so much, because he didn't deserve their love. One day they'd see him for what he was—a selfish, arrogant bully. But for now, they loved him. And as long as he didn't mistreat them, she needed to allow them to see him.

Despite everything, Tiffany now had a semblance of peace in her life. Leaving him had been the hardest thing she'd ever done, but she and the kids were far better off without him. Whatever insults or demands he might throw at her now couldn't affect her unless she let them.

But sometimes she still felt pathetic for not leaving before she did. How could she have endured so many years of being put down and manipulated by him? And how could she have put her children through it all? Even though he'd never hit them, they knew he hit her. What kind of a mother would allow them to witness that? Bile clogged her throat at the memories.

She got into her car and blew out several large breaths. Steve's response shouldn't have surprised her. She'd figure something out. One way or another, she'd manage to get Mike his boots.

After calming herself, she drove to one of the charity shops she liked to visit whenever she needed a new outfit. This time, she hoped they might have shoes to go with her dress. Her mother had given her a snippet of the fabric so she could colour match, but she was considering a contrasting colour as well. It all depended on what the store had in stock. Beggars couldn't be choosers.

When she arrived at the store, she was pleased to find they had several good options. In the end, she decided on a pair of silver pumps and a pair of elegant chandelier earrings. If ever there was an occasion to look her best, this ball was it. Although the total cost was reasonable, a wave of guilt flooded her as she paid for them.

How could she spend money on herself when she couldn't afford her son's football fees? How could she indulge in shoes and jewelry when she should be buying boots for Mike? For a brief moment, she considered putting both back.

"Great choices," the store clerk commented, looking at Tiffany with excitement as she laid the items on the counter. "Do you have somewhere fun you're going to?"

Tiffany blinked and gave a weak smile. "Yes, I do." Although she wasn't so sure it would be fun. More like eye opening.

"I'm sure you'll look beautiful," the girl said with a kind smile.

"Thank you," Tiffany replied graciously, but as she walked out of the store, she continued to debate with herself whether she should return the items. Perhaps she shouldn't be going to the ball at all. Had she made a mistake in accepting Marcus's invitation?

Although everything was sorted, no matter how hard she tried not to, she still worried about attending the ball with him, and now, here was another reason not to go.

She released a small breath. No, she'd told Marcus she'd go, and it was too late to change her mind. She'd go to the ball with him. It could be awkward and maybe even uncomfortable, but she'd go anyway. It would be good for her to get out of her comfort zone for once. Accompanying a handsome, rich man to a glitzy ball, surrounded by wealthy, exciting people? Surely she was allowed one evening of indulgence.

With that thought, she tossed her bag of goods into the car and indulged in one more extravagance by pulling into a drive-thru, where she ordered a frozen coffee drink. Normally, she preferred it simple, hot, and with nothing more than a little cream. But today she felt like something sugary and different, figuring she deserved it.

She sat in the car park and drank the coffee while enjoying the peace and quiet, but all too soon it was over. It was time to get the kids.

CHAPTER 10

It had been a busy morning and Marcus was looking forward to a break. The contract with Money Solutions was taking a great deal of time to finalise, and while it was going to be a great partnership, he was exhausted from looking at numbers.

Deciding he needed some fresh air he told his secretary he was going out. It was a pleasant day, warm but not hot, and the breeze was refreshing on his face. As he walked briskly along the footpath, his thoughts turned to his mum and how he wished she could still enjoy walks like this.

But then, out of nowhere, someone crashed into him from behind, nearly knocking him over. Regaining his balance before he hit the ground, he straightened and checked to see who had pushed into him.

He let out a groan. Sally. "Oh. Hi," he said, rather flatly.

Her arms were full of files. "Mark, I am so, so sorry! Are you okay? I didn't hurt you, did I?" she asked with concern dripping from her voice. A few spectators gathered around to watch the scene. Marcus felt a deep sense of discomfort and just a little annoyance.

It was late for her to be taking a lunch break, plus, there was no reason whatsoever for her to be carrying files outside the office building. What was she doing with them?

But he wasn't surprised. She seemed to be everywhere of late. He was beginning to question his own sanity and wondered if she was stalking him. That's what it was beginning to feel like.

"Sally, what files are those?" he asked bluntly.

She frowned and then looked down. "These?"

"Yes. Those."

"Well, I'm having a super busy day, but I needed to get a quick bite. My position in the company keeps me really busy so I thought I'd do some work while I ate."

Marcus couldn't help but sense that all of this was a lie and Sally was carrying those files for no other reason than to look important, and bumping into him was another way to get his attention. "You know there's a cafeteria in the building. On days when you're very busy, it might be a good idea to eat there. It'll save time if you don't have to leave the building."

For a moment, she looked like a frightened deer stunned by headlights before she replied. "The cafeteria doesn't have a lot of options for someone with gluten intolerance."

"Yes, they do. My secretary has a gluten intolerance, Sally. Quite a severe one, actually. She eats at the cafeteria most days."

He couldn't figure her out. He knew that Sally hadn't fully gotten over the trauma of having killed his father; that she

49

regretted using her phone and letting it distract her while she was driving. He wasn't oblivious to the fact that causing his father's death had affected her life. But that was no excuse for this strange behaviour. If she really ran into him on purpose, as he suspected, then things were starting to go too far.

"Well, I guess I should try the cafeteria again," she finally answered.

"Yes, I recommend it," he replied. "Have a nice day, Sally. And please bear in mind that we're legally bound to keep those files at the office for the sake of privacy. I suggest you head back right now and put them away and grab something to eat at the office."

She blinked nervously. "That's a really good idea. I was craving Thai food, though."

Marcus took two steps when he stopped again. He'd been planning to go to the nearest Thai restaurant. Had Sally been on her way to the same place? "Thai? You were after a Thai meal?"

"Yeah, you know the place on the next block? They have great food and the prices are reasonable." She let out a chuckle. "Not that that would worry you. Would you like to join me?"

He couldn't tell her that was where he'd been heading, but he was unwilling to lie. Quickly, he changed plans. "Sorry, I have a meeting soon, so I'm just grabbing a quick take-away from around the corner. But don't you think the Thai restaurant is a little far given you're in a rush?"

She shrugged and changed the topic. "How are your plans for the charity ball coming along?"

Marcus froze but managed a polite smile. "I'm going with a friend of mine."

"Oh really? That's great. A good friend?"

"A friend, Sally. Now, I have to insist that you return those files to the office immediately. If you're caught leaving with them again, your boss will have to issue a formal reprimand. Have a nice day." He nodded and strode away before she could continue the conversation.

He didn't like being rude, but it seemed she didn't understand him when he was polite. In the future, he would have to be firmer and make his point more insistently.

ALTHOUGH THE REST of the day passed in a flash, Marcus still managed to get home early as planned. He was hosting an event at his house for the youth of the church, and while not formally one of the youth group leaders, he tried to be involved in a lot of the activities which he also often funded.

The youth program at his church was wonderful. The leaders were truly committed to helping the young people grow into mature Christians who sought after Jesus. Rather than simply preaching about purity, the leaders taught them to seek Jesus above all else. Rather than only preaching about avoiding drugs, they offered them a way of doing that by placing their focus on living for Jesus and allowing Him to fill any void in their lives.

Once every quarter, Marcus opened his estate to the group. They could swim in the Olympic-sized pool complete with slides and water features, play tennis on the full-size courts, or hang out on his jetty. His yacht was out of bounds, although he occasionally took a number of the youth on it during the summer.

The kids loved the opportunity to go to the Alcott Estate and he was glad to have them.

He covered the cost of catering for these quarterly events. He'd learned early on that catering for youth was quite different than catering for adults, and rather than spending a fortune on small, fancy garnishes, he could order a few dozen pizzas and the kids were thrilled.

"You've pulled it off again," his friend David said, handing him a soft drink while they stood watching the forty plus kids enjoying themselves in the pool.

"They're a great bunch. You and Jeremy have really worked hard and your efforts are paying off," Marcus said, accepting the drink.

"I'm glad to hear you say that. You know, Jeremy is the best youth leader we've had at the church and I'm so glad I get to help out. It's a real privilege," David said humbly.

"You both do a lot of good work." Marcus gave his friend an encouraging smile.

"Thanks, Marcus. I appreciate that." He took a sip of his drink and then rested one hand against the wall. "We've been planning to start a new men's Bible study for guys specifically in our age group. We'd love it if you came."

Marcus had already heard a little about the group. He didn't think it was the place for him, but he appreciated the offer. All the men in David and Jeremy's study were married, and the thought of hearing them talk about their wives and families, as they no doubt would, didn't thrill him. Although he agreed he needed to do something. "Thanks, Dave. I'll give it some thought. The last study I went to was the one the church hosted on grief a few years back."

"That was a while ago, Marcus. I know you'll never fully recover from the loss of Bree, but don't make a hermit of yourself, okay?"

He wasn't a hermit. Marcus frowned. Is that what people thought? He interacted plenty at work. Maybe not so much at church. "I'll give it some thought."

"Good. Make sure you do." Dave clapped him on the back. "You'll never find another wife if you don't get out and about more."

Marcus was speechless for a moment. Dave meant well, but suggesting he was on the lookout for a new wife was insensitive. It fell into the same category as asking a newly married couple if they were pregnant yet. When he found his voice, Marcus had to comment. "What woman would want to spend her life in Bree's shadow?" he asked honestly.

"I agree. It'd take a very special woman, but they're out there. And there's nothing wrong with asking God to provide you with a special someone," David said gently.

Marcus didn't know quite what to say. He recognised the wisdom of Dave's words, but he also couldn't imagine his life with anyone other than Bree. She was the only woman for him. And without her, his life felt pointless at times.

Maybe that was the challenge and the evidence. Maybe the fact that he felt so lost without her was the very reason he should find someone to share his life with.

"I'll consider it," he finally said. He'd at least think about asking God to provide someone to share his life with. For now, that was the best he could offer.

CHAPTER 11

"That's perfect," Tiffany said, looking at the photo her sister showed her of the hair style she thought would look best on her. It was the evening of the ball, and Denise was helping her get ready at their parents' home.

Denise was a great hairdresser, and once more, Tiffany was thankful for having a dress maker in the family as well as a hairdresser who also enjoyed doing makeup.

It was saving her so much time, energy, and most importantly, money. She never would have been able to afford having her hair and makeup done professionally by someone else, and as someone who typically let her hair air dry and threw on a bit of mascara and little else, she wasn't quite the expert her sister was.

Of course, it was also a stroke of luck that her mum was not only a dressmaker, but one who happened to have enough fabric lying around from a previous project that she was able to make an entire dress out of it.

By the time Denise had completed her hair, Tiffany was thrilled. She could hardly believe her eyes when she saw the intricate updo in the mirror. "Okay, you need to do my hair more often," she said with a laugh.

"Tiff, *you* need to do your hair more often," her sister teased in reply. Tiffany couldn't help but laugh with her. She was fairly low maintenance, that was certain. But she was glad in that moment that she didn't have to rely on her own abilities.

"Now, go put on the dress," Denise insisted.

Tiffany carefully slipped the gown on, a figure-hugging A-line style that flared slightly from her hips, followed by her shoes and jewelry. She eyed herself approvingly in the full-length mirror, twirling this way and that. The dress was exquisite, and she felt like royalty. She'd never thought she could look so good.

Denise's mouth fell open. "Oh, my goodness! You look gorgeous!"

Tiffany laughed breathlessly. "I can't believe it either. Thank you so much." She gave her sister a hug as tears welled in her eyes.

"You're more than welcome." Denise held her at arm's length. "You look amazing, Tiff. Now, go show Mum. I think she'll burst into tears when she sees you."

"Okay." Tiffany blinked her own tears back. Holding up the bottom of the dress, she carefully went down the stairs, since she wasn't used to wearing heels and a full-length gown. When she reached the bottom, three sets of eyes stared at her. Mum's, Mike's and Polly's.

"Mummy! You look like a fairy princess!" Polly exclaimed loudly and with great enthusiasm.

"I couldn't have said it better myself." Her mum stood and gave her a hug.

A broad grin spread across Tiffany's face. It was truly a dream come true to feel so beautiful. If only she could bottle the feeling and hold onto it forever.

"Now, go on and have a wonderful night. Don't worry about the kids. You can pick them up in the morning after church and I'll only call in an emergency."

"Thanks, Mum." Tiffany kissed her mother tenderly on the cheek then turned to Mike and Polly. She wished she could get down to their level and look them in the face, but the dress made it impossible for fear of wrinkling or ripping the hem. Instead, she slipped an arm around each of their shoulders. "And you two be good for your grandmother, alright?"

Both children nodded vigorously and threw their arms around her waist. She wrapped her arms around them and kissed them goodbye when Denise announced that her ride was there.

Tiffany felt her heart leap into her throat, but she was ready to face the evening ahead, whatever it might hold. She glanced out the window. A stretch limo was parked in front of the house and she could hardly believe her eyes. Her magical evening had begun.

Stepping out of the house, Tiffany quickly realised she was on display for the entire street. Heads popped out of windows and doors, and her mother's neighbours stood in their front yards, pointing towards her and the limo.

As she made her way towards it, the driver, who'd been approaching the house, rushed back and opened the back passenger door for her.

She was already in the spotlight. Her pulse raced. Was she crazy for thinking this was a good idea? She hoped she was dressed appropriately. That she'd blend in and not be noticed.

Reaching the limo, she paused and turned around and waved to her family. They all wore grins on their faces, and her mother brushed her eyes and pulled the children closer. With another wave, Tiffany bid a final goodbye and stepped inside the limo to sink into a butter soft, white leather reclining armchair. .

She looked up and gave the driver a tentative smile. The kindly man, dressed in a dapper blue three-piece suit, removed his cap and gave her a reassuring nod. "Please make yourself comfortable, Miss Harris. If you need anything at all, press this button to speak with me and I'll attend to your needs immediately. And please help yourself to some refreshments which you'll find in the cooler."

"Th-thank you." Her voice squeaked. When he closed the door, she realized that she was shielded from all the stares of her family and spectators by the deeply tinted windows. Marcus was not in the limo, but she found a bouquet of roses with a note from him.

Dear Tiffany,

Thank you for accompanying me this evening. I hope it will be enjoyable for you as I'm sure it will be for me. The driver is picking you up first, but I will see you very soon.

Thank you,

Marcus

She read the note again. His tone was appropriate. Kind and friendly, but certainly not romantic in any way. She was grateful for that. The last thing she wanted was for any confusion between them. She was a date of convenience and nothing more.

And she hoped it would stay that way.

Although a small part of her wondered if there was anything deeper to Marcus Alcott's invitation, she tried to ignore that thought. It was ridiculous. There was no way a billionaire widower would want to date his mother's caregiver.

As the limo pulled away from the kerb, Tiffany settled back and enjoyed the ride. She'd sometimes wondered what the inside of a limo might be like. This one oozed luxury and elegance. Plush leather recliners with seating for perhaps ten people, a large plasma TV screen, a champagne bar, and a retractable roof. She'd never imagined such opulence could exist. If only Steve could see her now.

Soon the limo turned into the main driveway of the Alcott estate. She never entered via the front door, always using the back entrance which was more suitable for employees. But tonight she was a guest. Seeing the estate through fresh eyes, her breath caught. The circular driveway, surrounded by mani-cured rose gardens, was simply magnificent. *Had Marcus picked the roses from the garden?*

The limo stopped and Tiffany experienced a moment of panic. Should she wait? Should she go in? *What should she do?*

Those questions were answered quickly enough when the driver came around and opened her door. That was surely a sign she was to go to the house. She looked at the flowers and wondered whether she should take them with her, not really knowing if that was the right thing to do. Desperately trying to tamp down the anxiety that was building, she finally just grabbed the bunch before stepping out of the limo.

"Mr. Alcott is waiting for you inside, Miss Harris," the driver told her in a most polite tone. Once more, she felt quite certain he sensed her apprehension and was trying to put her at ease.

Nodding, Tiffany made her way to the front door of the mansion, careful not to tread on her gown. She pressed the buzzer and the door opened immediately. Her gaze met Marcus's. He must have seen her arrive, but she was surprised that he was the one who greeted her. The butler would normally answer the door. The sight of him in his black, trimly cut tuxedo pushed every thought away, except for realizing how lucky she was.

"Hi," he said, a shy smile spreading across his lips.

Tiffany hadn't expected to be quite so overwhelmed by his good looks, but she'd never seen him looking so elegant before. He was a handsome man, but something about him tonight took her completely by surprise.

"Hi," she replied, her voice almost squeaking again.

He leaned forward and kissed her on the cheek in a perfectly gentlemanly way. The kiss shocked her even more, but it solidified the fact that she was his date for the evening.

Tiffany felt herself blush, but she hoped he wouldn't notice, or that the layers of makeup her sister had added would cover up the pink. "Th-thank you. For the roses," she said, looking down at the flowers in her hand.

"Do you like them? I wasn't sure what flowers you might like, but it's hard to go wrong with red roses."

"They're beautiful." She gave him a sincere smile.

For a moment they stood awkwardly staring at each other

before he seemed to wake up to the fact that they were still in the doorway.

CHAPTER 12

$\mathcal{M}$arcus had not expected to be so entranced by Tiffany. She was exquisite in her navy gown. The sequins in the lace sparkled in the light, and her hair and accessories enhanced her overall outfit. He was sure she would catch every eye at the ball.

He'd always known she was a beautiful woman, but it hadn't been a thought he'd ever lingered on. She was his mother's caregiver so it hadn't occurred to him to think of her as more than that. Not when they only passed one another a few mornings a week for a matter of minutes. And certainly not when he was still grieving his wife.

But all of those things could not stop him from noticing her now. "Did you enjoy the limo?" he asked as they stood in the doorway.

"It was amazing. I've never been in one before, so it was a new experience. I think everything is going to be new this evening. I hope I don't embarrass you."

"I'm sure you'll be fine, and I'm glad to hear you enjoyed the ride," he replied with a smile. He could sense she'd been nervous at first, but within moments she seemed to relax a little. "Would you like to join me on the deck for a drink? We've still got some time before we have to leave."

She nodded. "That sounds great."

He led her through the house to the deck where a cart was filled with drinks. "What would you like? There are soft drinks, bottled mineral water, sparkling water, juice, wine or beer."

She hesitated. Maybe he'd given her too many options, but he'd wanted to be sure to have whatever she liked available.

"I'll have whatever you're having," she finally replied.

He nodded and smiled at her. "I'm having sparkling water with a dash of lemon. Is that alright?"

"That sounds perfect. And very refreshing," she replied with a laugh.

"Great," he said before getting to work making the drinks.

Despite not being a drinker, he always had an alcohol bar ready in case of meetings with clients or gatherings with employees for Christmas or other celebrations. A celebration would be expected soon after the closing of the new contract. He'd have to plan that at work during the next week.

But tonight was not a night to think about work, and he tried to remember that. It was a night to enjoy his time with a beautiful young woman and honour the memory of his late wife. It was a night to raise money so that no man would have to face the loss he had faced.

Nevertheless, Marcus couldn't help feeling a trifle guilty for being spellbound by this beautiful woman.

He hadn't been distracted by a woman in a very long time. No matter how many years had passed since Bree's death, he still considered her to be his wife, so to notice anyone else felt like a betrayal.

However, Bree wouldn't want him to still be grieving for her. He knew that in his heart. In fact, she'd told him not long before she passed that she wanted him to date other women after she'd gone. To fall in love. To marry. And yet, somehow it didn't seem right. Maybe it was still too soon. But he wasn't going to fall in love. Although Tiffany was a lovely woman, she was just doing him a favour by accompanying him to a ball.

Even if other people got the wrong idea about him bringing her, he was doing nothing wrong at all and shouldn't feel guilty. But nothing could develop between them, anyway, even if he did want it to. As far as he knew, she wasn't a believer, and that was the most important consideration for him. If she didn't share the same foundational beliefs as him, there was no point in considering the possibility of anything further.

It was strange to even consider such things, but he couldn't help thinking about the possibility of it developing into a relationship. Whatever he was feeling about Tiffany, he was thankful that she was willing to go with him that evening and they would enjoy their time together. It meant a lot that he had someone to take. Even better that she was gorgeous.

Handing her a drink, he sat beside her and gave a warm smile. "Are you comfortable out here? You're not cold?"

She returned his smile. "No, everything's perfect. And the view is amazing."

Marcus nodded. That was certainly true. The view was one of the best features of the estate, especially at this time of day as evening began to draw in and the lights across the harbour began to twinkle in the distance. Above them, the sky was turning from light blue to black, and a few stars began to pop out.

"You look fantastic, by the way," he remarked.

She turned to him, a look of gratitude and relief on her face.

"Thank you. Is it too much? I was a little worried I might be overdressed."

"Not at all. You'll fit in just fine." He didn't tell her that she might be the belle of the ball.

He sipped his drink and leaned forward. "I also wanted to thank you for joining me this evening, Tiffany. It's not easy trying to find a date for something like this, and I know it's probably a little awkward for you to be going with your client's son. But I'm truly grateful that you were willing to accompany me."

She lifted her gaze and met his. "I'm glad to be able to help. It was a little weird at first, being asked by you, but I'm glad you did. I think I need an evening out. It'll do me good to take a break from my normal life for one night and enjoy myself."

He smiled. "I'm glad to hear that."

They spent a few more minutes sipping their drinks and gazing out over the harbour in silence, but every now and then, Marcus snatched a glance of his enchanting date.

CHAPTER 13

*T*he view from the deck was incredible. Tiffany had never seen the harbour from this angle in the evening and she wondered what it must be like to actually own a home that had views like this from every aspect.

She'd been on the deck many times with Ruth, but never at night time with the lights across the harbour beginning to sparkle. And it was entirely different sharing the moment with Marcus. It was better than she could have imagined.

And then there was the fact that she felt like royalty. How could she possibly feel any more beautiful and wonderful than she did right now? It was all so perfect, she almost had to pinch herself to be sure it was happening.

For a moment, she had an urge to reach out and hold Marcus's hand, but she quickly snapped herself out of her daydream. This was not a real date. He'd politely clarified that when he thanked her for accompanying him. There was no reason at all to start imagining that there was anything more to the evening than that.

She couldn't allow herself to be distracted when there was nothing more to the evening than her simply accompanying him as they'd agreed. She barely knew him. Other than the fact that he was extremely rich, he worked at a tech company, and he had a great mum, she knew very little about Marcus Alcott.

She did know that he'd lost his wife to cancer, but not much else. No, she had to keep herself at arm's length and protect her heart. Keep the conversation on safe ground. She sipped her drink and then asked him about his work. "It's a tech company you work for, right?"

He faced her and nodded. "Yes, that's right. We host accounts for other companies and help them with their security, organisation, and systems. The company has grown into quite a large enterprise and we just secured a second major contract that's going to make us grow even larger. Of course, our small contracts are important, but it's the big ones that have gotten us this far."

Very little of that made much sense to Tiffany. She knew nothing about the tech world or what it meant to have contracts with other firms, but she was glad to hear that he was successful. She'd heard it was a very successful company, one of the top ten in the nation.

"So, what's your job exactly? I probably won't understand what it means, especially if it's some random techy thing," she laughed.

Marcus laughed in reply. "Well, I started out as a programmer, helping to build some of our software. But then I moved up, and finally, Bree and I bought the company from my former boss. He was a great ideas man, but he didn't have the skills to take the company further."

She was confused. Did that mean he owned the company? "Wait, you mean, you're the CEO?"

He shrugged, as if almost apologizing. She saw no mock surprise or false embarrassment. He was completely genuine when he nodded. "Yes, we bought it just over ten years ago, not long before my father died, when it was still a small enterprise. We took on a number of small contracts, and then, six years ago, the company snagged this major contract with a national travel company. It's taken time to adjust to that growth and ensure that we were ready to take on another huge project."

Tiffany still couldn't believe that Marcus owned the company. She had no idea. She felt like a fool for not having known and wished she could take back the irrelevant questions she'd asked. "Wow. I had no idea. I knew you had a great position there, but I had no idea you were the owner," she said, hesitant to meet his gaze.

How was it that she was going to an event with a man who was not only extremely wealthy, but who actually owned a multi-billion-dollar business? "So how does one go from being a programmer to a CEO?" she inquired further, in awe of his achievement.

"Well, I studied IT and got a minor in Business Management in school. Then I got a dual MBA and a Masters in programming. So, with those two skill sets, it seemed reasonable that I should use them both. It's funny, though, the smoother the business runs, the more obsolete I become. We have a large staff now. For a while there, I was only going into the office for meetings several times a week."

"You were only working a few days a week?" She frowned. Why hadn't she known that? She laughed to herself. The mansion was so large he could be home and she wouldn't know it.

"Yes. But over the past few weeks while we've been negotiating this new contract, I've become busy again."

"What made you decide to buy your former boss's business?"

Marcus sighed with a sad smile. "My wife and I talked and prayed about it for a long time. My boss had mentioned that he was considering selling and he wanted the right person to take over, but Bree and I weren't sure if we wanted to spend that much money to buy him out. We had very little in those days. But after praying about it a lot, we felt that everything pointed to us going ahead and taking the leap."

"Wow. I bet you're glad you decided to do it."

"Very. It's just sad Bree's not here to see what it's become."

"I'm so sorry. I shouldn't have pried."

"It's okay. Anyway, tell me about your kids. Mike and… what's your daughter's name again? Sorry."

"No problem. It's Polly. Mike's ten and Polly's eight."

"Ten and eight. You're so lucky." A winsome look crossed his face. She knew he didn't have any children and wondered if he and his wife had wanted any.

She nodded. "I think I'm in the good years right now, though," she said, fixing her gaze on a yacht sailing by. "I'm not looking forward to them being teenagers, especially now that I'm on my own."

"I can only imagine how hard parenting alone must be. What are they doing this evening while you're out?"

"They're with my parents. They love having the kids, and it's good for Mike and Polly to spend time with their grandparents. My older sister isn't married yet, although she's engaged, so Mike and Polly are the only grandkids and my folks adore them."

"My sister has three children and my mum adores them, too, as you probably know. I'm sure she talks about them a lot."

Tiffany smiled. "Yes, she does." Ruth talked about them often, and photos of the three filled the living room.

Marcus glanced at his watch. "It's about time to leave. Would you like another drink before we go?"

"No, I'm good, thanks." Having relaxed significantly since arriving, she was now looking forward to spending the evening with him. Still, she had to remind herself that this was not a date. Marcus Alcott was CEO of a multi-billion-dollar company and she was just the woman who cared for his mother. Their date was nothing more than a date of convenience. She would have to be okay with that, even if she was suddenly noticing him.

He stood and she followed suit, taking the flowers that she'd set down beside her.

"I really hope you enjoy the evening," he said as they walked through the house and made their way towards the front door.

Before she could reply, Ruth approached in her wheelchair. Tiffany hadn't seen her and hadn't even known she was in the house. Perhaps she'd wanted to give them time alone.

"Sorry for the intrusion," she said. "I just wanted to wish you both well and tell you that I hope you have a wonderful evening."

Tiffany smiled before leaning over and giving her a hug. "Thank you. I'm sure we will."

"You're more than welcome. And my goodness, Tiffany, you look amazing! I love your dress." She kept hold of Tiffany's hand.

Tiffany smiled. "Thank you. My mum made it."

"Well, she did a splendid job. She must be a wonderful seamstress."

"She is," Tiffany replied with pride.

"You take good care of this girl, Marcus," Ruth said, squeezing Tiffany's hand.

"I will. Don't you worry about that." He leaned down and kissed her cheek. "We have to go, Mum. Good night."

"Good night, dear."

As they continued towards the front door, Ruth called after them, once more wishing them a pleasant evening. Tiffany's heart beat out a staccato as they left the house and strolled towards the limo. Marcus had placed his hand lightly at her waist. She was sure it was simply out of politeness, but she couldn't help the tingle that raced through her body at the touch of his hand. She felt as if she was in a fairy tale as they got into the limousine and it drove away.

The evening had already started out so magical; she couldn't imagine what might lie ahead.

CHAPTER 14

The limo pulled up to the Ritz Hotel at Darling Harbour and Marcus took a deep breath. He'd been to many events here, including the past three years of the charity ball which had been hosted at the hotel. From the expression on Tiffany's face it was clear and evident that she was impressed by the glitz and glamour.

She rolled down the window and eyed the view. A number of limos were ahead of theirs, and one by one they released their passengers and drove away.

"It's amazing," she said, awe in her voice.

"Wait until you see the inside."

She looked at him with wide eyes and he sensed she'd grown a little anxious.

"I should probably give you a heads up as to what to expect."

She nodded. "That might be helpful. Thank you."

"Well, I'm one of the main benefactors," he began.

"Of course you are." She chuckled, rolling her eyes teasingly.

He laughed in reply, although he wished he could express to her how truly unimportant he was in the grand scheme of things. He might be one of the main benefactors, but the real stars of the evening were those who'd battled cancer and survived. They'd been through so much, and he felt honoured to be able to support the foundation financially, because it truly was making a difference.

"Well, yes. So, as a benefactor, we'll be paid quite a lot of attention. But don't worry. No one will bother you and I'll be with you the whole time unless, of course, you feel comfortable enough to talk to people on your own. Otherwise, all you have to do is stay by my side."

"Stay by your side and I'll be fine?" she asked, echoing him.

"Exactly. I won't leave you on your own unless you want me to. But..." he said, leaning in close, "if you want to chat up any other men, at least try to keep it subtle."

Tiffany laughed. She seemed to appreciate his attempt to lighten the moment. He was glad the joke had landed well.

"I promise I'll ask for their numbers discreetly," she teased.

"Perfect," he replied, smiling. He was pleased that even with the serious chat they'd had on the deck, they'd managed to start off the evening fairly light-hearted.

There was something about her laugh that he truly appreciated, and it warmed him. She was a unique woman and one he was glad to have by his side.

"What else does a main benefactor get? Any special privileges? Do you get to steal stuff from the hotel?" she asked light-heartedly.

He chuckled. "All the time. I have a collection of pure silver candlesticks now. I take one every year." His reply elicited more laughter from her.

The jokes were not overly clever, but it was still a relief to think he had something to offer other than his arm. Finally, their limo reached the front of the line and the driver came around to let them out.

Stepping onto the pavement, Marcus watched Tiffany's face light up as she gazed at the hotel. He offered his arm, which she took, and as they made their way up the stairs, he could tell her sense of wonderment increased with every step.

The doors were held open by hotel employees who bowed and greeted them as if they were royalty. Placing his other hand on hers, he gave a squeeze of encouragement. She glanced at him and gave a grateful smile.

When they reached the main hall, her eyes widened, but hers weren't the only ones. As she admired the room, others admired her. The gazes of more than a few men were on Tiffany. A number of the older women raised their brows, while others offered smiles of admiration. Marcus thought it best not to point these things out to her, lest she grow self-conscious, but it was clear to him that he was with the most beautiful woman in the room.

Entering the expansive ballroom, Marcus greeted each of the guests he knew. "Mr. Hamilton, very nice to see you. How have you been?" he asked, shaking the elderly man's hand.

"Excellent. Last week was five years since I got my all-clear," the man replied with a look of pure joy.

Marcus congratulated him and introduced him to Tiffany.

"My goodness, you are quite the beauty. And you've got a

good man on your arm tonight, young lady. When Marcus helped cover the costs of my third surgery, I vowed to be as generous with my money as he was until the day I died. Of course, at that time, I thought death was much nearer, but alas, now I'm held to my word," he said with a chuckle.

Tiffany shot Marcus a sidewise glance and lifted a brow.

He shrugged. What else could he do?

He greeted a number of other guests, many of whom were cancer survivors, or loved ones of those who didn't survive. By the time they found their table, Tiffany leaned into him and whispered, "I suppose nothing should surprise me anymore, but you really are quite the philanthropist."

Smiling, he replied, "I'm only using my resources the way they should be used. I figure God wouldn't have given them to me if He didn't intend me to do something beneficial with them."

She nodded a little awkwardly, as if she didn't understand the concept, but Marcus didn't mind sharing bits and pieces about God throughout the evening if it meant opening a door for them to talk more in depth at another point. In the meantime, he was glad that she seemed to be enjoying herself and was certainly more comfortable than he had anticipated.

He looked around the room again, as he did frequently in case there was anyone he'd missed greeting. For the most part, general mingling would cover most of his acquaintances, and then after the organised events, there would be more time to chat with the guests. But he truly wanted to ensure he was not rude to anyone, especially as these were honoured guests, recipients of the foundation's endeavours, or donors like him who sought to be generous with their finances and time.

As he gazed around the room, a flash of black caught his eye. A young woman with a short, black bob, thick rimmed glasses, and a similar body type to Sally Hubbard stood across the room, wearing a black dress that wasn't quite the standard of the evening.

He blinked, and just as quickly as he saw her, she was gone.

Could it have been Sally? Had all his run-ins with her made him paranoid?

Thousands of women in the world had that same haircut and dark hair. There was no reason to start panicking and making assumptions. Sally was a lost young woman. Not a stalker. He had to stop interpreting her behaviour as anything more than that.

Besides, the room was filling up with people of different races, ages, styles, heights and body types. There was bound to be someone in the crowd who looked similar to her.

Marcus decided to relax and not worry so much. He didn't have to constantly be on alert. He looked at Tiffany who was conversing with the woman who'd just sat down next to them. Glad she appeared so comfortable, he chose to focus on enjoying the evening with the woman who had unexpectedly captured his attention, and not on some imaginary stalker.

Before long, everyone had taken their seats, and their table had filled with other important benefactors and people he knew well. It was time to introduce them all to Tiffany and let her shine.

CHAPTER 15

*F*eeling slightly overwhelmed, Tiffany held onto Marcus's arm until they were seated. Once settled, she tried to make polite conversation with the woman beside her, but her gaze kept darting to Marcus.

The whole event was foreign and slightly challenging for her, but for him, it was as if he were just having friends over for dinner.

His calm demeanour helped her relax, and soon she felt she was handling herself quite well.

"Amelia," Marcus greeted and then stood to hug a woman who'd approached their table.

Tiffany followed suit and stood, ready to greet the glamourous woman with a high, black-haired bun and show-stopping golden gown. Tiffany guessed she was quite elderly, but she carried her age with dignity. Amelia was striking and it was evident that she was important.

"Amelia, this is Tiffany Harris," Marcus said, introducing the two.

Amelia extended her hand. Tiffany took it before the woman gave her a kiss on each cheek. She tried not to snicker. Rich people actually did this at fancy events!

"My goodness, Marcus, she puts the rest of us to shame! And your dress. Tiffany, you simply must tell me all of your secrets because you look magnificent. Not only that, but well done for convincing Marcus to bring you to this do." Amelia winked at Marcus and let out a small chuckle.

Tiffany smiled but was unsure how to interpret Amelia's statement. Did she think that Tiffany had invited herself and she was after Marcus? Before she could stop herself, she said, "Well, it wasn't me, but rather his mother who convinced him to invite me." She gulped. Maybe she shouldn't have said that. Was it proper to talk about things like that at events like this?

"Of course! Ruth is quite the persuasive woman, isn't she?" Amelia replied.

Tiffany sighed with relief. "She certainly is. She had to convince both of us that this would be a good idea. I think I rather got the better end of the deal," Tiffany joked, glancing coyly at Marcus.

"Oh, Marcus, she is just perfect!" Amelia exclaimed.

Tiffany felt her cheeks warm. The older woman's words flattered and encouraged, but also caused embarrassment. Was she giving Marcus the wrong impression?

After briefly discussing the schedule with him, Amelia made her way to the next table, promising to return. There were still two empty seats and Tiffany assumed they belonged to Amelia and whomever her partner might be.

"That's Amelia Donovan." Marcus finally had a chance to explain. "She has an amazing, huge personality, as you can tell. Her husband, Timothy, has a heart of gold, but is very nearly silent. His wife does all the talking, and honestly, she does it well. They're the managing directors of the research foundation."

The explanation was helpful for Tiffany, who wanted to understand the context of everything that was occurring. "It's helpful to know that," she replied. "Are they scientists looking for a cure?"

Marcus frowned and shook his head. "Fifteen years ago, their sixteen-year-old daughter became sick. They lost her within four months of her diagnosis. Not long after that, they set up the trust."

"She was only sixteen?" Tiffany gasped softly. She'd never heard of someone so young dying from breast cancer.

"Yes. She was an extremely rare case, but it happens. They established the foundation and they host this charity ball every year to raise more funds for research. They'll be sitting at our table, but they have to say hello to everybody first," he continued.

Tiffany nodded solemnly. She couldn't imagine the amount of loss felt by the people in this room. Nearly all those present had either survived breast cancer or lost someone to it. Or, like one of the men Marcus had talked to, had suffered other forms of cancer. It seemed the worst of tragedies.

Marcus ensured she was properly introduced to everyone at the table and included small pieces of information about them. There was little for him to say when introducing her, but she didn't mind that so much. She liked her privacy and didn't mind appearing a bit mysterious. And compared to what they'd all been through, her situation paled in insignificance. Nevertheless, she enjoyed meeting her dinner companions. The conversations shifted about, but primarily focused on the evening at hand.

Considering she'd never experienced anything remotely like this event before, she was surprised by how comfortable she felt with everyone.

Julia, another of the women at the table, raved about her dress and Tiffany couldn't wait to tell her mother what a hit it was. She was glad to know that her mum's talents and abilities were being praised by women who wore outfits that probably cost thousands.

"Believe it or not, it's a one of a kind from a very small-town designer," Tiffany said, hiding a grin.

"Oh? Who is she? I simply have to get the designer's number," Julia replied with excitement.

"Well, her name is Marjorie Watson, but I like to call her mum," Tiffany said with a wink.

Julia's mouth dropped. "Are you serious? I'm entirely jealous. How lucky you are!"

"I know. She makes a lot of dresses and has been in the business for more than thirty years, but she's never taken her skills beyond school dances and bridesmaids. I keep telling her she should branch out, but she lacks a little confidence," Tiffany added.

"Well, tell her she should. Do you have any idea how many women have been staring at your gown tonight?" Julia asked.

At Julia's request, Tiffany provided her with her mother's information, and as the night wore on, several other women also asked for her details. She couldn't help but beam with pride and was excited for the possibility of her mum getting work from women who ran in these circles. It was certainly going to be a surprise for her.

Marcus was busily entertaining people, but when others came around, he introduced her with increasing pride. At one point, she caught him looking at her with sparkling eyes. He leaned over with a smile and said, "I'm impressed."

Tiffany tilted her head. "Oh? By what?"

"How at ease you look."

Tiffany felt her heart race. His compliment was as smooth and genuine as his voice. Smiling in appreciation, she replied, "Thank you."

Their gazes met and held. Something in his look mesmerised Tiffany, and her heart thumped against her ribs. She held his gaze for what seemed an eternity.

Just then, someone on the stage announced that the event had raised a significant amount of money and all of the donors were thanked. Tiffany tore her gaze from Marcus and gulped while joining in with the applause when he was one of five given special acknowledgement for the work they'd done on behalf of the charity.

While the applause sounded and Marcus stood and humbly acknowledged the honour, Tiffany saw him in a new light, and a new and unexpected warmth surged through her.

CHAPTER 16

*T*he ball came to an official close. The entire evening had been wonderful, and Marcus couldn't have chosen a better companion. Tiffany had handled herself with grace and dignity he'd not expected, and when they danced and he felt her body close to his, old forgotten feelings had been rekindled. Try as he might to not be attracted to her, he knew he could very easily fall for her.

As the guests and patrons slowly began to leave, he could see that Tiffany was unsure what to expect next. It was getting late, but he wasn't tired and he didn't need to go home. In fact, the event had ended sooner than anticipated, by at least a half hour. He placed his hand lightly on her back as they headed towards the exit and asked her softly, "Would you like to take a walk along the harbour, or would you prefer to go home?"

She hesitated a moment, but then smiled and said a walk sounded lovely.

He was relieved, and if he were honest, he was pleased their time together would be extended. She'd impressed him so much throughout the evening, and he felt that a slender delicate thread had begun to form between them.

Strolling the short distance to the harbour, a light breeze wafted across the water and Marcus felt entirely content.

"You know, your mum is an amazing woman," Tiffany said unexpectedly.

He hadn't known what they would talk about, but he hadn't expected his mother to be the first topic. His mum *was* an amazing woman and it was nice hearing her complimented and respected. He turned his head and nodded. "Yes, she is."

"There's something about her, the way she sees the world and how positive she is. She always has something good to say to everyone, and she's always thinking of others even though she's continually in pain. If only more people in the world were like her."

Marcus smiled. "That about sums up my mum. She's a woman of faith who lives her life for God no matter how she's feeling. It's her faith that leads her to treat others so well."

"She does talk a lot about God."

"He's very important to her. She and my dad raised my sister and me in the faith as well. We're both Christians, and I'm thankful for the upbringing we had." He didn't want Tiffany to feel uncomfortable, but he wanted her to know, that just like his mum, his faith was also a big part of his life. Although he'd begun to feel an attraction towards her, it was a non-negotiable for him. He couldn't be with a woman who didn't share the same beliefs.

"So, faith is important to you, too?" she asked, sounding a little confused.

He nodded. "Extremely."

She grew quiet and he sensed she wasn't overly impressed with his response. Finally, she responded, "So, if you don't mind my asking, how can you believe that God cares? I mean, with everything you heard tonight. All those stories of heartache and death. How can you believe there's a loving God?"

He drew a slow breath. It was a reasonable question, and one he'd also asked when Bree died. Reaching the end of the walkway, he stopped and leaned against the railing. Tiffany stopped and stood beside him. On the opposite side of the harbour, lights twinkled, and the sound of water lapping against the pylons below was soothing. He let out a deep sigh. It was hard to understand how a loving God could allow so much suffering when it was in His power to stop it, but he'd come to learn and accept that God's ways were higher than his, and that in this life there were no straight answers. It took faith to believe, but he knew beyond a doubt that this life was just a stepping-stone to eternity where everything would become clear. "You know my wife died of breast cancer?"

Tiffany visibly winced as she nodded. "Sorry, I guess I shouldn't have brought that up."

"No, that's not what I mean. I'm not upset you mentioned it, but I asked the same question you just asked when she was suffering in pain. I was a Christian, and so was Bree, but when I watched her suffer, and then when I experienced such grief when she finally passed, I begged God to remind me that He was real, and that He truly loved us just as I'd been taught, because I'd started to doubt." He rubbed the back of his neck with his hand and met her gaze.

"But God never promised us that life would be easy. Death happens. That's what Adam and Eve were warned about before they sinned. But they sinned anyway, and death was a direct result of their disobedience.

"I know that for Bree, death was a relief and I'm confident she's now pain free in the arms of Jesus. She suffered a lot before she passed, but now she's better off than you or me. We see things from our finite perspective only. We don't want our loved ones to die, but we fail to see that death is a stepping-stone into a whole new world, and that for someone suffering such pain, it's a wonderful release if they know Jesus."

Tiffany looked perplexed. He was far from a theologian, but at the very least, he could share his own personal story with her.

"My parents are Christians," she said quietly.

"They are?"

"Yes. They're not as devout as your mum, but they go to church most weeks. When I was young, I used to go, too. But I stopped going when I met Steve."

Marcus could hear the pain in her voice as she spoke his name. Her ex-husband must have treated her very badly, and it grieved him. "Have you been back to church since?"

"I've taken the kids a couple of times, at Christmas and Easter, mainly." She turned and gazed over the water, twisting her hands together over the railing. "I never saw much truth in the Bible. It seemed more like an excuse for people to make themselves feel better, and with everything I've seen around me, it's hard to accept that God cares at all."

Marcus nodded. "The world is certainly full of suffering,

but that doesn't mean it's a lost cause and we should lose hope. God does care, and there's always hope."

Turning, Tiffany looked at him steadily, and he couldn't help being captivated by her eyes. He'd not noticed how clear and blue they were until now. He would have to firmly remember his resolve. Tiffany was not a believer and he couldn't let himself develop feelings for her. But that didn't mean he couldn't be her friend.

CHAPTER 17

*S*tanding beside Marcus, gazing into his soft, brown eyes, Tiffany drank in the nearness of him. She was surprised by how easily she'd come to look at him in this way, but she quickly pulled her gaze away and looked instead across the water. She couldn't let this happen. She couldn't let her heart get broken again. Because, surely it would if she fell for him.

"So, tell me about your children," he said, as if sensing a change of subject was needed.

She smiled. She loved talking about her children and bragging about them to anyone willing to listen. "They're the best. Mike's a typical ten-year-old boy. He loves to mess around and cause trouble, but never more trouble than I can handle. And he's already starting to eat like a teenager. He loves pizza but isn't fond of vegetables."

"I can relate to that. Mum still has trouble getting me to eat my veggies." Marcus chuckled and she laughed along with him, grateful for the way he was able to lighten any conversation.

"And Polly?"

Tiffany smiled as she thought about her daughter. "She's a girly girl but pretends not to be. I think she'd give just about anything to have Mike play dress-up with her, but instead, she puts on her jeans and tries to keep up with him and his friends." It was nice talking about her children, and Marcus seemed truly interested in them.

"They sound like great kids. I get to help with the youth at church, but it must be amazing having your own children."

"It really is. I'm very lucky, and I never take them for granted."

Marcus remained silent for a moment and then asked her a personal question. "What happened to their dad?" he asked tentatively.

Tiffany gave a half-smile and a subtle wince.

"You don't have to talk about it," he said.

"No, it's fine." She twiddled a lock of hair between her fingers as she felt his gaze on her. "I've been free of him for four years now. Steve and I were married for seven years, and the emotional and verbal abuse started just after we got married, but even then, I believed I was nothing without him." She gave Marcus a sideways glance; his eyes were gentle, caring. She generally didn't like sharing about her marriage, but she felt comfortable with him, and he'd also shared about the loss of his wife, and she knew that mustn't have been easy.

She blew out a heavy breath. "It was right after I had Mike, a year into the marriage, that the physical abuse began. It turned out that Steve wasn't ready to be a father and he took his frustrations and anger out on me, which was better than him letting them out on Mike. I should have left then. If only I'd been stronger." And that was the truth. She'd felt caught and unable to stand up to him, so she'd stayed.

"I had no idea you'd gone through all of that. I'm so sorry, Tiffany." Marcus spoke with compassion, but there was nothing about his tone that made her feel pitied or ashamed. He was good at saying the right thing.

She turned and faced him. "It's okay. I eventually stood up to him and finally managed to leave. It wasn't easy, but it made me a stronger person."

"I can see that. You're a very strong woman."

She drew a breath. She might be, but being strong continuously was tiring. She never wanted to be vulnerable again, but she couldn't help pondering what it would be like to be with a man who truly loved and cared for her and didn't try to control her. Somebody like Marcus…

No, she needed to push these unexpected feelings and thoughts back where they belonged. She'd only get hurt if she let herself indulge in them.

Over the course of the evening, his caring attitude and genuine interest in everyone he met had truly impressed her. She even admired the sincerity of his faith. It was a strange topic for her to be thinking about. After all, with everything she'd gone through with Steve, she'd been convinced that God couldn't truly care about her, or that He didn't exist at all. But it seemed that, like his mother, Marcus took his faith seriously and that could be why he was so humble and kind.

Despite her resolve, when she once again felt his gaze on her, there was a tingling in the pit of her stomach.

CHAPTER 18

$\mathcal{M}$arcus held back, although he wanted to draw closer to Tiffany and comfort her. She'd gone through so much. He wanted to hear more of her story and share more of his own with her. His heart had begun to swell with feelings he'd thought were long dead.

But growing close to Tiffany wasn't an option. They could be friends, nothing more. Not only for his own sake, but for the example he was setting for the youth at church. He'd encouraged the young men not to be swayed by women who weren't believers. He'd told them about Bree and how their marriage had been blessed because they held the same beliefs.

Although he couldn't deny the attraction he felt for Tiffany, he couldn't disregard what he knew to be true and right. He had to hold fast to what he believed, and he needed to rein in his feelings.

Finding himself considering her as anything more than a friend was completely unexpected. Until tonight, he hadn't thought of another woman romantically since Bree passed. What had triggered these feelings? The romance of the evening, or seeing Tiffany in a totally different light? She'd certainly dazzled not only him, but all those at the ball.

No, he felt quite certain it was none of those things. It was *her*. Her strength. Her spunk. The way she'd handled herself with grace and confidence in an unfamiliar situation. The way she spoke of her children.

He held her gaze and felt his resolve weakening. She was beautiful, inside and out, and he could easily fall for her. Gulping, he ran his hands down his slacks. "I should call for the car, it's getting late."

"Yes." She grabbed his hand. "Thanks for the evening, Marcus. I know your mum suggested you invite me, but I'm really glad you did."

He swallowed hard. "I'm glad, too." He had to stop there. She was growing on him more than he cared to admit.

He called the driver and within moments, the limo arrived. The driver opened the door and Marcus stood back to let Tiffany in first. He slid in beside her, casting her a sideways glance as the limo took off, and offered her a drink.

While they drank coffee and listened to soft music playing through the speakers, Marcus couldn't remember the last time he'd enjoyed an evening quite so much.

Arriving outside Tiffany's home, he got out and walked her to the front door where he turned and faced her. "Thank you again for coming with me tonight."

"And thank you again for inviting me." Her smile threatened to disarm him.

"I'll know who to call if I need another date for one of these dos," he laughed.

"I can't promise I'd wear a different gown." She chuckled and then grew serious. "I really enjoyed the evening, Marcus. Thank you." He thought he saw longing in her eyes, and he swallowed hard.

"So did I, but I won't keep you any longer." As he gazed into her eyes, he was tempted to kiss her cheek. Instead he took her hand and lifted it to his lips. "Good night, Tiffany."

"Good night, Marcus."

After returning to the limo, Marcus replayed the events of the evening in his head as he sat in the back on his own. He'd not expected to be drawn to his mother's caregiver, but Tiffany's strength and determination had taken him unawares, and the harder he tried to ignore the attraction he felt for her, the more it persisted.

The limo pulled into the estate, and after thanking the driver, Marcus went inside and checked on his mum. She didn't stir as he opened the door quietly. She was another strong woman. Despite her frailty, when she needed to do something, she did it. Even getting from her wheelchair into her bed was not easy for her to do without help, but somehow, she managed it.

She'd lived ten years without his dad, her husband, longer than Marcus had been married to Bree. But she'd not only overcome her loneliness, she'd determined not to let bitterness rule her life, and had instead forgiven Sally, the young woman who'd caused her husband's untimely death.

The remembrance of his father's accident sparked curiosity in Marcus again. Had it been Sally he'd seen at the ball? He hoped not. He didn't want to think she was stalking him, and he didn't know what it would mean if she were. Surely Sally wasn't dangerous, just strange and awkward.

He was growing weary of her and wished she would keep her distance. She made him deeply uncomfortable at times, but it seemed there was little he could do. However, right now, he was exhausted and Sally was the last thing he wanted to think about.

Climbing into bed a short while later, Marcus thanked God for the wonderful evening, and he also prayed a blessing on Tiffany, his unexpectedly alluring, gorgeous date.

CHAPTER 19

*A*few days later, after dropping the kids at school, Tiffany made her way to the Alcott Estate. Ruth was hosting the weekly Bible study in her home this week and had asked her to help with the preparations after attending to her personal needs. She'd also invited her to stay for it.

Since the evening of the ball, thoughts of God had flitted through Tiffany's mind, but the idea of sitting with a bunch of ladies studying the Bible made her feel uncomfortable. She hadn't promised to stay, and now she was thinking she'd attend to Ruth and then make an excuse to leave.

She hadn't heard from Marcus. While she hadn't expected him to call, she was disappointed. She couldn't forget the way her heart beat fast as he'd lifted her hand and kissed it gently; it was the most romantic moment she'd ever experienced, and she hadn't been able to sleep for hours afterwards. Steve had never had that effect on her. Ever. But maybe she'd only imagined a connection between her and Marcus.

Because of all this, Tiffany was anxious to face Ruth. She drove her car around the back and as she crossed the gravel to the back entrance, she paused and took in the view of the harbour. Memories of the evening with Marcus flashed through her mind. Had it all been a dream? Had she really sat on the deck with him and chatted while sipping their drinks? It seemed so unreal now, like a fairy tale. How silly to have allowed hope of anything more to grow inside her. Things like that didn't happen in real life, not for women like her, anyway. She was his mother's caregiver. They'd had a date of convenience. There was nothing more to it than that.

"Tiffany! I wondered if I'd see you before I left."

Her eyes widened. Wearing a dark grey business suit and looking as handsome as ever, Marcus stepped out the door and approached her. "I was just about to leave for work. How are you?" His broad smile made her heart flutter.

"Great, thanks." Returning his smile, she tried hard to keep her voice steady.

"Thanks again for coming with me the other evening." He spoke sincerely, but she sensed caution in his voice.

"You're more than welcome." Why did their conversation suddenly seem stilted? They'd chatted so easily the night of the ball. "I'd best go in. Your mum will be waiting for me. She invited me to attend the Bible study this morning." *Why did she say that? She hadn't planned to stay.*

"Really? I'm sure you'll enjoy it. Mum loves her study group."

Tiffany shrugged. "We'll see."

"I have to go, too. Enjoy your day, Tiffany." He gave her a warm smile before leaving.

She paused before going inside. Seeing Marcus again, she felt like she was swimming through a haze of feelings and desires. She should have known this would happen. If she hadn't gone with him to the ball, she wouldn't have this dull ache inside her. Nothing could develop between them. He was a billionaire and she was his mother's caregiver. She couldn't afford to harbor any romantic notions—she had to put them away right now before she went inside.

Ruth was in her bedroom. Tiffany knocked softly and entered when Ruth looked up and smiled. "Tiffany, how are you? How did you enjoy the ball?" Her voice oozed sweetness, and Tiffany wondered what Marcus had told her.

She was determined not to let Ruth see the war of emotions raging within her. "I'm good, thanks. And the ball was amazing." Tiffany walked over to where Ruth was seated on her oatmeal coloured, mid-century Scandinavian armchair in front of the large bay window.

"Marcus said you dazzled the crowd." Ruth's eyes twinkled.

Tiffany bit her lip. *What else had he said?* "I'm not quite sure about that, but it felt nice being dressed up."

"Well, I'm glad you enjoyed yourself, my dear." Ruth reached out and patted her hand. "Now you'd best help me prepare for the morning. I don't want to greet my guests in my nightgown!"

Tiffany chuckled and got about her work. Caring for Ruth Alcott was never difficult; Ruth always put Tiffany at ease and made her feel better about herself. As Tiffany brushed Ruth's hair, she decided that she'd stay for the study after all. Not because of Marcus. Not because of Ruth. She'd stay for herself.

Maybe she could find some answers to the questions she'd been internalizing.

Ruth's friends began to arrive, and Ruth greeted them warmly and introduced them to Tiffany. They gathered in the morning room where a table was laden with freshly baked cookies and pastries. Tiffany was by far the youngest woman in the group, but the ladies were friendly and kind and included her in their conversations while sipping their tea.

Soon, Ruth cleared her throat and drew the group to attention. "Thank you all for coming this morning, and a special welcome to my caregiver, Tiffany." Ruth turned to her, and with a warm smile, she patted Tiffany's hand. "I'm delighted she's joining us today."

The group of ten ladies all nodded and smiled at her. With all the attention, Tiffany felt herself growing a little anxious but smiled back.

"Shall we make a start by asking the Lord to bless our time together?" Ruth asked the group.

Once again, the ladies nodded and then bowed their heads. Seated beside Ruth, Tiffany followed suit. It had been a long time since she'd closed her eyes in prayer, and something inside her shifted as Ruth prayed quietly.

"Dear Lord, we thank You for being here with us today. Please bless our time together and may our hearts be open to Your word. Let us be touched by what we read and learn, and help us to become more like You. In Jesus' precious name. Amen."

A round of quiet *amens* followed and then they all opened their Bibles. Ruth handed Tiffany one.

"Last week we finished Romans seven, and this week we're

on to Romans eight, which you all know is my favourite," Ruth said with a small chuckle.

The women quickly flipped through the pages of their Bibles to find the book and chapter. Tiffany had no idea where to find either. She was relieved when Ruth discreetly located it for her.

"Who would like to read the first verse?" Ruth asked.

A woman to Tiffany's left said she would. She read the verse slowly and carefully. "'Therefore, there is now no condemnation for those who are in Christ Jesus.'"

Condemnation. Such an intimidating word. Exactly how Tiffany had felt most of her life, or at least since she left home. She'd suffered Steve's condemnation for most of their marriage, and she'd continued to condemn herself for not leaving before she did and for allowing her children to stay in that environment for too long.

And yet, here was this verse, saying that there was no condemnation in Jesus.

Tiffany listened intently as Ruth and the women discussed this verse and those that followed. For many years, she'd thought God was punishing her. She'd been certain that all the hardships she'd suffered were punishment for disobeying her parents and leaving the church when she met Steve. But these verses were saying that for those who loved God, there was freedom from condemnation, sin and death. God loved her as a precious child, and nothing could separate her from that love.

In that moment, Tiffany came to realise that truth was not dependent upon experience. She'd been condemning herself when there was no need. For so many years she'd taken the blame for her failed marriage and had over-compensated by trying too hard to give the children what she thought they needed, but maybe, all they needed was her love. And for her to be free of guilt.

Later that day, after returning home, she mulled over that morning's discussion. The Bible study might not have changed her views completely, but it had been enough to make her start thinking.

CHAPTER 20

*T*hat night, while eating dinner together, Ruth once again asked Marcus about the ball.

"I've already told you, Mum, it was a wonderful evening," he replied, wondering if perhaps she'd started forgetting things.

She leaned forward and tapped his hand. "Yes, but I'm asking about Tiffany. Did you have a nice time with Tiffany?"

"Yes, of course we had a nice time. She was a great companion."

"I'm only asking again because of this morning's Bible study. She seemed more open to the gospel than she's been before, and I wondered why that might be."

Marcus's interest was piqued. The whole day at work he'd been curious about how the Bible study had gone and whether Tiffany had enjoyed it, so this was certainly interesting news. "Oh really?" he replied.

"I think she's really searching," his mum said while trying without success to twirl some spaghetti onto her fork.

"Let me help, Mum." He hated seeing her struggle so, but she always insisted on trying to do things herself.

"Thank you, dear. I don't know what I'd do without you."

He smiled as he took her plate and cut the spaghetti into small pieces to make it more manageable. "That's great to hear about Tiffany. We did chat about God the other night, so maybe it got her thinking. I'm not sure." Since the evening of the ball, he'd prayed daily for Tiffany. He couldn't get her out of his mind or his heart. She'd changed something in him— shown him that he could care about a woman again, and that was a major step forward. But nothing could develop between them unless she shared his faith, and he wasn't sure if he'd been praying for her for selfish reasons, or because he truly wanted her to know the love of God in her life for her own sake, regardless of whether anything developed between them or not.

"I think you and Tiffany should spend more time together," his mother announced.

Marcus continued cutting the spaghetti and held in his surprise. Since she'd suggested he invite Tiffany to the ball, he guessed she was trying to match make them, so he simply answered, "And why's that?"

"Because I think you would be good for her. You know, she really is wanting to know more about God. I can see it in her. I don't know her full story, but I've sensed from little things she's said that she doesn't entirely trust men. I think you could change that."

"She has good reason not to trust men, Mum. And I don't think that my being around her a whole lot is going to fix that. She needs to learn to trust God first, and I think that you and your Bible study ladies could probably help with that more than I could."

"I'm not trying to force anything on you, but it would be nice for you to spend time with a woman who makes you happy, and I believe Tiffany does." Her eyes twinkled mischievously.

Marcus chuckled as he handed the plate back to her. "Are you finally admitting that you're trying to set us up?"

She remained silent for a moment before shrugging. "Okay, I admit it. But I'm right, Marcus. I know she's not a Christian, and rushing into a relationship isn't a good idea, but there's no harm in getting to know her and being her friend. You never know what might develop, especially since she seems open to the gospel."

Marcus twirled some spaghetti onto his fork. These were the thoughts he'd been trying to avoid. What if he spent time with her and fell in love, but she decided not to believe? What would he do then? Could he go against his own beliefs and principles, or would he be strong enough to end the relationship, hurting not only himself, but possibly Tiffany as well?

"I truly don't think I should encourage anything at the moment, Mum. I do like her, but I don't want either of us to get hurt. I'll pray for her and I'll be friendly, but I don't think it would do either of us any good to take things further right now."

His mum nodded. "I was afraid you might think that way,

and you're probably right. However, I believe the two of you would make the most wonderful couple, so I'm not going to give up."

Marcus laughed. "I didn't expect you to!"

CHAPTER 21

*T*he Bible study had caused Tiffany to think about her life and what she believed. She'd always considered herself to be a good person, and she believed that as long as she tried her best to be kind to everyone, that was all that mattered. But after hearing those Bible verses and the ensuing discussion amongst the ladies, and then realising that she'd been punishing herself for years over the failure of her marriage, she suddenly felt tired. Tired of striving to prove she was a worthy mother, tired of trying to prove to Steve that she could raise their children on her own, tired of doing life without God. Suddenly, she'd come to accept that He did care, just like Marcus said He did.

By the time she saw Ruth again, she had a ton of questions for her elderly client. Arriving a few minutes early, she wondered if she might see Marcus. Try as she might, she couldn't shake his image from her mind, but her hopes were dashed. His car wasn't in the garage. Although she knew a relationship with him was impossible, she couldn't stop her heart racing every time she thought of him.

Tiffany let herself into the house through the back entrance and looked for Ruth. She wasn't in the morning room or the kitchen, so Tiffany made her way to her bedroom and tentatively knocked on the door. "Ruth, are you there? It's me, Tiffany."

"Come in, dear." Ruth's voice sounded frailer than usual.

When Tiffany pushed the door open and entered, Ruth smiled. She was sitting up in bed reading.

"Good morning, Ruth. Are you not feeling well?" Tiffany asked with concern as she approached the bed. Rarely did Ruth Alcott stay in bed beyond seven, despite there being no need for her to rise that early.

"I'm fine, dear. I just decided to stay in bed and read until you arrived. Marcus brought me breakfast before he left." She put her book down and patted the chair beside her. "Come and sit down."

Normally, Ruth would be eager to have Tiffany help her dress, not sit and chat in her room. Nevertheless, Tiffany did what she requested and eased herself into the most comfortable armchair she'd ever sat in. She loved Ruth's bedroom, and she occasionally let herself daydream about decorating her own room in a similar style, but it was very much only a daydream since she couldn't even afford to buy football boots for her son.

Tiffany guessed that Marcus had opened the floor to ceiling drapes and the French doors leading onto the balcony where Ruth often sat. Dappled sunlight poured in, highlighting the wedding photo on Ruth's mahogany dresser. Each time Tiffany looked at the photo she felt a pang in her heart. Ruth and her husband looked so young and in love. She felt so sad for Ruth losing her husband when she so clearly still loved him. Tiffany let out a sigh. She and Steve had also been young and in love once, but unlike her client's marriage, theirs had ended badly.

"What's on your mind, dear?" Ruth asked softly.

Tiffany blinked. It seemed Ruth could read her mind. She shrugged. "I… er…I'm not sure." But that wasn't quite true. She was sick of the struggle inside her and the confused thoughts and feelings that had been assailing her of late.

"Is it Marcus?"

Tiffany shook her head. "No." That wasn't quite the truth, but how could she confess to his mother that her son had captured her heart?

Ruth patted her hand. "Well. If it's not Marcus, what is it?"

Tiffany inhaled deeply. "I've been thinking about the Bible study."

Ruth's face lit up. "That's wonderful, dear! Would you like to talk about it?"

Tiffany tugged a piece of hair and wrapped it around her finger. "I think so. But I'm not sure where to start."

"That's okay. We've got all day. Why don't you help me dress and we can sit outside and chat over coffee?"

Nodding, Tiffany smiled. She was fortunate to have such a caring and empathetic employer. After helping Ruth out of bed, she assisted her with a shower and getting dressed before pushing her through the massive house, stopping in the kitchen to make coffee before proceeding outside to the deck.

The harbour looked magnificent. With barely a breath of wind, the water was as still as a millpond and as blue as the sky above. A hovercraft skimmed across the water before slowing and pulling into a jetty, and overhead, a plane soared across the sky, leaving a trail of vapour behind it. Tiffany doubted she would ever tire of the view.

She placed a cushion behind Ruth's back and poured the coffee before sitting on a wicker armchair. Sipping her coffee, she tried to relax, but so much was going on inside her that she began to feel overwhelmed. She thought she'd had it all together, that she was strong and could manage life on her own, but she was realising that what she needed was to let her walls down and become vulnerable. Not in a bad way, but in a way that let people see the real her—the woman who'd thought she had it together but couldn't afford football boots for her son. Not the strong woman she presented to the world.

Feeling tears welling behind her eyes, she glanced away, hoping Ruth hadn't noticed, but it was too late. Ruth handed her a tissue. "What's the matter, dear?"

Tiffany grabbed the tissue and wiped her eyes. "I don't know. I've just got all this stuff swirling around inside my head and I don't know what to do about it."

"I'm happy to listen."

Tiffany smiled. "Thank you." She sniffed and blew her nose.

"Drink your coffee, dear. There's no hurry."

Tiffany nodded and reached for her cup. Coffee was what she needed, and as the hot liquid slid down her throat, she felt herself grow calmer. After taking several sips, she told Ruth how she was feeling. That she felt like she'd failed and she was tired. Tired of struggling. Tired of life.

Ruth rubbed her back. "Jesus said, *'Come to me, all you who are weary and burdened, and I will give you rest.'*"

Tiffany gave a weak smile. "That sounds wonderful, however, all these years I've thought religion was only for people who don't have the strength to take responsibility for their own lives." Wincing, she patted Ruth's hand. "Not you or Marcus, of course, nor my parents, but people in general. I've always thought a person should be self-reliant and not depend on anyone, not even God, to get through, so it's really hard for me to accept that I need someone else in my life."

"I can understand that, dear. Many people believe that, but it doesn't mean it's right. The Bible says that humankind is created by God and made in His image. He knows each of us intimately and it grieves Him when people choose to live their lives without Him. Loving Him and having a relationship with Him isn't a crutch; it's the only way to have a truly meaningful life. I'm sure you've heard the quote, 'There's a God-shaped vacuum in the heart of each man which cannot be satisfied by any created thing but only by God the Creator, made known through Jesus Christ'?"

"I think I've heard it," Tiffany said. "It's hard for me to let go of what I've believed for so long, but I somehow think that the God-shaped vacuum inside of me is wanting to be filled."

"My dear girl, that's wonderful." Ruth smiled as she squeezed her hand. "Giving your life to God isn't something you should do lightly. It's a life-changing decision, but one you'll never regret."

"Will you explain to me what it involves?" Tiffany couldn't believe she was having this conversation. Since leaving the church when she started dating Steve, religion had meant nothing to her, but something was happening inside her she couldn't ignore, like an awakening of sorts, and all of a sudden she had an urge, *a need*, to know more about God.

"With pleasure." Ruth grinned. "I suggest we set aside some time each day you come here, and we can study the Bible together. I don't want you making a decision before you're ready, but I sense God is drawing you to Himself, and if you have an open heart, I don't think it will be long. Can I pray for you, my dear?"

Tiffany wiped her eyes and nodded.

Ruth placed her hand lightly on Tiffany's back and began. "Lord God, thank You for my precious friend, Tiffany. She's such a special woman and I know You love her dearly. Open the eyes of her heart that she might see You. Let her see that giving her life to You isn't a sign of weakness, but instead, it's like coming home. Wrap Your arms around her and fill her with Your peace as she seeks for truth. I pray all these things in Jesus' precious name. Amen."

Tiffany raised her head and hugged Ruth as she fought back tears. "Thank you. I appreciate that so much."

"You're more than welcome, my dear. Now, shall we make a start?"

"Yes, please. But before we do, let me make another coffee for us both."

"Great idea! And bring out the carrot cake when you return."

"Now that's an even better idea." Tiffany laughed as she stood and picked up the tray. "I'll be right back."

"Take your time. There's no hurry."

Tiffany walked back inside the house to the kitchen that was larger than her entire home. She'd always admired the

Italian marble counter tops and the top-end European appliances, items she would never be able to afford, but today she barely noticed them as she poured two mugs of fresh coffee. Everything inside her was tingling with anticipation now that she'd admitted her need. She couldn't wait to start her study with Ruth.

Returning soon after with fresh mugs of coffee and a slice of carrot cake each, Tiffany sat beside Ruth and waited eagerly for her lesson to begin.

As Ruth shared the gospel message with her that day, Tiffany knew that her life was about to change.

CHAPTER 22

*A*t work, Marcus was filling in a spreadsheet and scratched his head. Some of the estimated costs were higher than expected, mainly under the miscellaneous expense column. It didn't sit right with him.

Pressing his finger to the intercom button on his phone, he spoke to his secretary. "Stephanie, can you see if Mr. Waitts is available to come in this afternoon for a brief meeting?"

"Yes, Mr. Alcott. Certainly. I'll call right now."

"Thanks, Stephanie. You're the best."

"The best? Really?" came a voice at the door of his office.

Marcus looked up and groaned. Sally was peeking through the crack in the door.

He kept his face as blank as possible. Since Sally tended not to understand facial cues easily, he didn't want her thinking he was pleased to see her, but he also didn't want to offend her entirely.

"Sally, do you have business to discuss?" he asked in a business-like manner.

"Of course, I'm all business," she replied as she pushed the door open and invited herself in. Her hips swayed suggestively as she stepped forward.

Marcus sat back in his chair and folded his arms, fixing her with a steady gaze. "Have your supervisor bring me anything that's necessary. You know I don't work directly with employees since that would mean going over their supervisor's head. That's not the way we do things here, Sally. We follow that command structure."

"Well, my business isn't entirely work related," she said, batting her dark lashes.

A small breath blew from his mouth. His attempts at remaining neutral were fading fast and he just wanted her out of his office, but instead, she slinked closer and sat across from him, crossing her legs so that a flash of thigh was obvious.

"Sally, this isn't appropriate."

"What? I'm not allowed to visit a friend?" she asked, rolling her bottom lip out in a fake pout.

"I'm going to ask you a straightforward question," he said, leaning forward and placing his elbows on his desk.

"Okay, go for it. I'm an honest person," she replied, also leaning forward, giving him an eyeful of cleavage.

Marcus's gaze jerked up and he cleared his throat. "Good. Tell me the truth. Were you at the charity ball on Saturday night?"

Sally's face went blank. Several beats ticked by before she finally responded. "Well, I said I'd be honest, so you should know." A coy smile flitted across her lips. "Of course, I was there. I wanted to see you receiving all those honours."

His suspicions had been correct. Sally really had followed him to the ball. Anger seething inside him, he took some deep breaths to avoid saying things he might regret. "You need to leave my office, immediately, and please don't return. This behaviour is not okay, Sally. It's deeply inappropriate. Can't you see that?"

"I don't understand." She crossed her arms and frowned.

"I'm uncomfortable with your behaviour. You need to leave me and my mother alone, okay? It's not okay to follow me outside the office and flirt with me at work or anywhere else," he repeated.

She glanced away but didn't move. His response had hurt her, but he couldn't allow himself to be sensitive to her feelings just then. He had to be firm. She was not in a healthy state of mind, it seemed, but he couldn't condone this behaviour. Especially in the workplace.

"Well, I understand," she said, standing. "You just haven't realised yet that I'm the one for you. You haven't recognised the love we could share, but I have. It's only a matter of time before you do, too. And when you do, you'll be begging for me to come back to you."

With those words, she finally turned and walked away slowly, pausing to look over her shoulder, as if giving him a chance to call after her, beg her to stop, to come back to him.

She really believed what she was saying.

Chills ran down his back and his gut churned. The woman was unstable. How could she possibly believe they were supposed to be together?

Sally needed help, but his mother had tried before and she'd refused. He felt at a loss. He just wanted her out of his life.

As important as forgiveness was, stalking was another matter altogether. Sally was growing erratic. She'd followed him to the charity ball. How had she even managed to get a ticket? Had she stolen one? Or had she saved every penny from every paycheck to buy one? The charity ball was not an inexpensive event. The whole point was to raise money.

Redirecting his thoughts, Marcus focused on the best part of the ball. Tiffany.

A buzz from his intercom disturbed his thoughts. It was his secretary advising him that Mr. Waitts would arrive within the hour. Marcus busied himself prepping everything for the meeting and for a while, he forgot about both Sally and Tiffany.

He had a lot on his mind. Between the contract with the business, his feelings for Tiffany, and trying to sort out what to do about Sally, he felt overwhelmed, so after sorting the issue with the budget, which proved to be nothing more than an incorrectly inputted figure, he decided not to go straight home. He called his mother and told her he would be a little late.

"But I have something exciting to tell you," she said, disappointment ringing in her voice.

"I'll be back before you go to bed. I just need to do something," he said as he held his phone between his shoulder and ear while packing up his computer.

"Alright then, but don't be too late," she said, resigned.

Marcus found her tone somewhat strange. Normally his mother didn't mind so much when he was late, but she seemed extra bothered about it today. He wondered what the exciting news was and decided he'd better not dally too long.

Hurrying out of the office, he prayed he wouldn't bump into Sally, and after getting into his BMW, he headed directly for the cemetery where Bree's body lay. Normally he visited once a week. He knew she wasn't there, but her grave was a tangible thread between them, and visiting helped him cope. Kind friends had suggested he decrease his visits to speed up the healing process, but it wasn't easy to do that. And now, with his growing feelings for Tiffany, he needed to visit Bree's grave more than ever.

The cemetery overlooked the ocean, and as darkness drew in, he paused to breathe in the salty sea air. Below, waves crashed against the rocks and seagulls squawked overhead. Bree had loved the ocean, one of the reasons she'd chosen to be buried here. How he missed her. He walked on, and reaching her grave, stopped and stood before the headstone.

But for the first time, he found it wasn't Bree he needed to talk to. It was God. After spending a few moments at her grave, he returned to the cemetery's entrance. Sitting on a bench seat, gazing out at the ocean with wind whipping through his hair, he unloaded his heart to God.

By the time he ended, he felt a deep sense of peace. Although he had no idea how his future would unfold, he knew he could trust his Creator to be with him and guide him in every aspect of his life.

WHEN HE ARRIVED home and his mother told him that Tiffany

had given her life to the Lord, he uttered a prayer of thanks while a wave of emotion rushed through him. Could this be God answering his prayers already? Was there a chance their friendship could develop into something more? He dared to hope it might.

CHAPTER 23

Two days had passed since Tiffany had given her heart to the Lord. She couldn't explain it fully, but she felt different inside. Ruth had told her that when she said yes to Jesus, not only were her sins forgiven and she was free from condemnation, but she also received the Holy Spirit, and from that moment on, her life would begin to change from the inside out. She already felt that happening. The Bible had started to come alive for her, and she found she was eager to read it more and more as the words spoke to her heart.

When she told her parents that she'd given her life to Christ, they were overjoyed and said they'd been praying for her every day since she stopped going to church.

Tiffany was leaving Mrs. Honeycutt's home just before midday when her phone rang. She fumbled in her bag, and when she pulled it out, her eyes widened. It was Marcus. She swallowed hard before answering, "Hello?"

"Tiffany, it's Marcus." His voice was deep and smooth and sent a ripple of anticipation through her.

"Hi! How are you doing?" She cringed and rolled her eyes. Couldn't she come up with anything better than that?

"I'm doing well, thank you. I hope this isn't a bad time, but I wanted to ask you something."

"Okay…" she responded.

"Would you and your children like to join my mum and me for dinner on Friday evening?"

She blinked, speechless. Marcus was asking her to dinner? And not just her. Mike and Polly as well. Was she dreaming? She was too startled by his invitation to respond immediately.

"Are you there?" he asked.

"Y-yes," she replied, quickly gathering her composure. "Dinner sounds great. I'd love to join you, and the kids will be thrilled."

"Tell them to bring their swimsuits. They're more than welcome to use the pool."

"They'll be so excited," she said, trying without success to keep her voice steady.

"Great! Shall we make it six o'clock?"

"Sounds good to me."

"Oh, there's another thing…" He sounded a little unsure of himself. "Mum didn't go into details, but she mentioned that you prayed with her and that you accepted Jesus. I'm so happy for you, Tiffany, and I was wondering if you'd like to come to church with me on Sunday."

Goodness! This was almost too much. Marcus Alcott, handsome billionaire, had not only invited her and her kids to dinner, but to church as well. She couldn't believe it. But she couldn't allow herself to be distracted by romantic notions. He was most likely just being kind. Her parents had invited her to attend church with them, but if she were honest, going with Marcus was way more appealing. Throwing caution to the wind, she accepted.

"I'd love to go with you, and I'm sure the kids will enjoy it as well. Thank you so much for inviting us."

"Wonderful. Then I'll see you on Friday and we can talk about Sunday then. Does that work for you?" His voice was soft now.

"Yes, it's perfect, thank you."

After the call ended, Tiffany sat in her car in a daze. Where had her resolve gone? How had she so quickly accepted his invitations? Despite the chemistry between them, she'd determined not to allow herself to fall for him. They were from different worlds. How could anything eventuate between them? And yet, she felt a sense of peace flowing through her. *Is this the peace Ruth talked about, Lord? Is it truly okay for me to have accepted Marcus's invitation?*

She didn't receive a response, but she would have been surprised if she had. God didn't talk to people directly these days, did He? It was all new to her, this praying thing, but she didn't think He did. Not out loud, anyway. Closing her eyes, she continued to pray.

I'm out of my depth here, Lord, and I have no idea of where this might go, but I ask You to lead and guide me and give me wisdom. I don't want to be hurt again, and I don't want my children to be hurt, either. But if You arranged this, thank You! I honestly can't believe it. It's beyond my wildest dreams, and even if Marcus only wants to be friends and nothing more, it's still amazing.

Starting her engine, she headed back to the office on cloud nine.

On Friday evening, Tiffany was corralling the kids into the car when Polly looked up at her and said in her sweet, innocent voice, "Mummy, you look beautiful tonight."

"Thank you, sweetheart." Tiffany felt her cheeks warm. She'd only put a little blusher and lip gloss on and put her hair up, but Polly had obviously noticed. Although she'd reminded herself it was not a date, it was simply dinner with her employer and her client, she sensed that it was actually more than that. Or it could be. Why else would he have invited her? Something tangible had definitely happened between them on the night of the ball that she couldn't deny or ignore. She just hoped she wasn't about to get hurt again.

"Your hair is really shiny too. You look pretty," Polly continued.

Tiffany bent down and hugged her. There was something about Polly's innocence that brought tears to her eyes. Despite all she'd been through, she was such a well-adjusted, happy little girl. And she was really into shiny hair these days since her friend gave her glittery hairspray. Tiffany blinked back tears and stifled a chuckle.

Arriving at the estate, Tiffany hesitated. She felt uncomfortable driving into the circular driveway and parking her old Hyundai in front of the main entrance, but that's what Marcus had told her to do. She was his guest, he'd said. Park out front. Okay... she stopped the car under the portico.

"Is this one of those fancy hotels where a doorman comes

out and parks the car for us?" Mike asked excitedly, leaning forward in his seat.

Tiffany held back a chuckle. "No, it's not." She didn't say she'd be embarrassed for anyone else to drive her car, but she thought it. "Mr. Alcott told me to park out here. I normally park around the back when I come to look after his mother."

"Can we go swimming right away?"

Tiffany turned her head and glared at him. "I told you to be on your best behaviour. You can go swimming when Mr. Alcott says you can, and not before. And don't go asking him, okay?"

Mike slumped back against the seat. "Okay."

"Come on then, let's get out, and make sure you don't touch anything."

"We won't," both children said simultaneously.

"Good." She'd had a long talk with them about their manners and not touching anything in the house, but she was anxious about them breaking one of Ruth's Ming vases or knocking into Marcus's marble statues. They wouldn't do it on purpose, but they were kids, and accidents happened. But she didn't want them walking on eggshells all night, either. It was awkward for all three of them.

They climbed out of the car and Tiffany locked it, more out of habit than anything. No one would want to steal her car in this neighbourhood, that was for sure. Polly slipped her hand into hers and walked close beside her, but Mike walked one step behind, as if he wanted to maintain a bit of independence. Tiffany could understand that. She probably would have done the same in his shoes. Stepping onto the flagstones outside the double front door, a wave of apprehension swept through her.

What were they doing here? Maybe they should turn around and go home. Her heart thudded in her throat.

"Can I ring the doorbell, Mummy?" Polly asked.

Tiffany fought her apprehension and nodded. "Okay. But ring it only once."

"Okay." Polly raised her hand and was about to press the buzzer when the door opened.

Marcus stood before them wearing a tan coloured button-up shirt with black trousers and smelling of exotic cologne. Their gazes met and her pulse throbbed double-time. He exuded masculinity.

"Hello there!" he said, lowering his gaze to the children and smiling at them. "I'm Marcus. And you must be Mike and Polly."

"Mum said we are to call you Mr. Alcott," Mike said.

"Did she just?" Marcus let out a small chuckle and lifted his gaze to Tiffany's, his eyes glinting with amusement.

She shrugged. "I want my kids to be respectful of the adults they meet."

"I'm happy for them to call me Marcus if you're comfortable with that."

"Yes, I'm okay with it." She smiled and placed her hands lightly on each of the children's shoulders. "They're very excited to be here."

"Well, come on in. Mum's waiting to meet them, too. She's out on the deck catching the last of the sun." He ushered them in and walked with them through the foyer and down the hallway. Tiffany was aware of both Mike and Polly turning their heads to gaze at the rooms they passed. She imagined their mouths dropping open as they passed the main living room with its designer furniture, huge chandelier, and plush velvet drapes. She was certain it was the most impressive room they'd ever seen.

When they reached the deck, Ruth looked up, her wrinkled face creasing in a smile. "Tiffany! How nice to see you. And your children! At last I get to meet you. Come here and let me look at you." She held out her arms.

Sensing their hesitation, Tiffany pressed their backs more firmly. "Children, this is Mrs. Alcott. Say hello."

"Hello," they said in unison.

"It's so nice to meet you at last. Your mother has told me so much about you."

Once again, Tiffany sensed they weren't sure what to say. Relief flowed through her when Ruth added, "And it's all good! Now, I'm sure you'll want to go swimming. Marcus has arranged for a couple of the youth from church to supervise you, unless of course you'd like to stay here with the adults."

They looked at each other and then looked questioningly at Tiffany.

"If you'd like to go swimming, that's okay," she assured them.

"I can take them down if you like. Dinner isn't until seven, so they'll have plenty of time to swim before then," Marcus said.

"That sounds great. Thank you."

"Go with them, Tiffany. You don't need to stay here with me," Ruth said, waving her away.

"As long as you're sure." Tiffany could tell that Ruth was contriving to push her and Marcus together, but to be honest, she really didn't mind. She realized again just how attractive Marcus was and was anxious to spend time with him.

"I'm sure." Ruth's tone left no room for argument.

"Okay then. Thank you." She smiled at Ruth and then turned to Marcus. "They're wearing their swimmers so there's no need for them to get changed."

"Great. Let's go." He led the way down the flagstone path, passing the summer house complete with a spa and a gymnasium, until finally reaching the pool.

"Wow!" Mike exclaimed. "Look at all those slides! Can we go on them, Mum?"

Tiffany laughed. "As long as Mr. Alcott, sorry, *Marcus*, says you can."

"That's fine by me," he replied. "Jack and Susie are going down a slide now. Come with me and I'll introduce you."

They followed him to the far side of the pool and waited for the pair to splash into the water. The kids laughed when they got wet.

Jack and Susie emerged and quickly climbed out. Marcus made the introductions and then he and Tiffany stood and watched as the pair, whom Tiffany guessed were in their late teens, took her children under their wings.

"They seem like nice kids," Tiffany said.

"Yes, they're brother and sister, and they're great with younger children since they have three younger siblings."

"It's very kind of them to offer to supervise my two."

Marcus laughed. "They'd do anything to come over for a swim."

"Right." She could imagine that. What kid wouldn't want to swim here? The pool was amazing.

"Would you like to take a walk?" Marcus inquired.

"Yes, I would." She smiled and once again felt her heart pounding as memories of the night of the ball flashed through her mind.

"You have lovely grounds," she said as they strolled along pathways filled with scented shrubs and colourful annuals. The perfume of gardenias wafted in the air, and she ran her hand through the lavender bordering the pathway and brought it to her nose, breathing in the heady scent.

"Thank you. We have a great gardener who keeps it in top shape." A few moments later, he said, "I really was glad to hear about your decision."

Tiffany smiled. "I am too. It's amazing to think that the truth was there all along, waiting for me. To know that thousands of years ago, Jesus was thinking of me and it's only been two days since I realised what that means. I'm thankful for your mum, for explaining everything to me so well." She paused and glanced at him. "And for you. The things you said started me thinking."

"That was my pleasure, Tiffany. I'm glad it helped."

"So am I. The past two days have been life changing. At your mother's suggestion, I've read through the four Gospels and also Acts and Romans. I need to go back and read them more slowly, but I just couldn't stop once I started."

Marcus's brows lifted. "You've read all of that in two days?"

"I know. It's weird, but I'm desperate to know more. But as much as I want to read about Jesus, I'm already excited to read the Old Testament as well. I watched a sermon online about how important it is not to separate the two."

Marcus shook his head and chuckled lightly. "It's not weird. It's amazing. I hope your passion for scripture never wavers."

"Me too."

Stopping when they reached the jetty, they stood side by side and gazed out at the harbour. As the sun slowly slipped over the horizon, washing the sky with soft pinks and oranges, Tiffany felt at peace with herself and with God. Whatever was happening with her and Marcus was in His hands.

A little later, she sat and chatted with Ruth while Marcus finished preparing dinner. She learned that he was an excellent cook and had even considered becoming a chef when he was young. When they all gathered around the table, she quickly realised why.

He'd been slow-cooking a side of lamb on the rotisserie since early afternoon and it was cooked to perfection, and the vegetables were to die for. Mike even ate the honey-roasted Brussel sprouts without a fuss. Soft dinner music played quietly in the background while they ate, and Tiffany kept pinching herself to know she wasn't dreaming.

After a dessert of creme brûlée, Marcus asked Mike and Polly if they'd like a hit of tennis.

"But we don't know how to play," Polly said sadly.

"That's okay. I can give you some pointers."

"Okay then," she said brightly.

"How about you, Tiffany? Would you like a game?" He swung his gaze to hers.

Her heart fluttered as their gazes connected. She chuckled a little nervously. "After that meal, I don't think I can walk, let alone run."

"We can take it easy. It'll be fine." His voice was as soft as silk.

"Alright then. But I haven't played in years."

"No problem. Neither have I." He winked, sending her pulse skittering.

"If you don't mind, I think I'll give it a miss," Ruth said with a laugh.

"That's fine, Mum, but you're welcome to watch," he said.

"No, I think I'll do a spot of reading."

"Okay. We won't be long." He bent down and kissed her cheek.

The next hour was filled with fun and laughter, and then, a little later, while the kids watched a video, Marcus and Tiffany sat on the deck overlooking the harbour, sipping tonic water with lime and mint.

"It's been a wonderful evening. Thank you, Marcus," she said.

"I'm glad you've enjoyed it, because I have, too." He turned to face her and a tremor ran through her body at the passion in his eyes. "If it's not too premature, would you have dinner with me again next Friday? Not here, though. And just us. A date. A real date."

Her heart danced with excitement. A date! A real one. Before she knew it, the answer flew out of her mouth. "Yes! I'd love to."

CHAPTER 24

$\mathcal{H}$e was almost late, but Marcus pulled into Tiffany's driveway just in time to pick her and the kids up for church. He hadn't been to her house before, but he wasn't surprised by how neat and tidy the small front yard was. He knew she was a hard worker, and he guessed that trait flowed through to every aspect of her life.

Polly was running down the steps before he managed to get out of the car. He laughed when she ran right up to his door and spoke to him through the window. "Thank you very much for taking us to church, Mr. Marcus. I like going with Grandma and Grandpa, but it will be fun going in your big car."

"You're more than welcome, Miss Polly."

A flash of blue caught his eye and he looked up at the house. Dressed in a simple, blue floral dress, Tiffany had come out with Mike and was closing the door. Her dress, although simple, accentuated her slim figure. With the sun shining on her pinned up hair, she looked gorgeous.

He quickly opened his door, taking care not to knock into Polly, and climbed out. Walking towards Tiffany, he greeted her with a smile.

Tiffany returned his smile as she approached with Mike. "Good morning." Her gentle voice floated in the air.

"Hi! I hope you don't mind sitting in the back. Mum's in the front."

"That's fine," she replied.

He opened the back door and the kids climbed in. Before she followed them, their gazes met, and he was once again entranced by her subtle beauty.

Soon they were on their way. The conversation was light and simple during the short drive and when they reached the church, Marcus helped his mum into her wheelchair. Tiffany offered to push. Once inside, Marcus said he'd take the kids to the Sunday school hall.

"Are you sure? I'm happy to take them," Tiffany said.

"It's fine. Why don't you stay here with Mum?"

"Okay." She gave him a warm smile and then sat. He took the kids to the Sunday school hall and signed them in. He wasn't blind to the looks he received from some of the women, but instead of explaining, he simply smiled at them.

On his way back to the sanctuary, Dave walked beside him. "You've got a looker there, mate," he said, winking.

Marcus shot his friend a warning look.

"Sorry, I didn't mean to be so crass. I'm glad you've found someone at last, Marcus."

"We're only friends," Marcus said, but even to himself, he didn't sound convincing.

"I've heard that one before." Dave chuckled and clapped him on the back. "It's all good, Marcus. You'll have to introduce me."

Marcus smiled. "Okay. After the service."

The worship band had begun playing by the time he reached his mum and Tiffany. Sliding past his mum, he stood beside Tiffany, casting her a quick glance before turning his focus to the words of the first song.

Throughout the service, he couldn't help but glance at her every now and then. He struggled to believe that she was here with him, in church, and that she now shared his faith. It was an answer to prayer, and he was truly grateful.

When the service was over, his mum said she'd wait in the foyer and chat with her friends while he and Tiffany collected Mike and Polly.

Reaching the Sunday school hall, Jocelyn, the head teacher, frowned. "Did the kids forget something?"

"No. We're here to pick them up," he replied.

Her face clouded as she glanced at Tiffany and then back at him. "What do you mean, you're here to pick them up?"

Marcus was confused. It was a straightforward statement, after all. "We've come to collect the children from Sunday school," he replied, trying not to grow annoyed.

"Marcus, their mum already came for them," Jocelyn said, glancing again at Tiffany. Her expression grew more puzzled.

"*This* is their mum, Jocelyn." He placed his hand lightly on Tiffany's back.

Jocelyn looked around nervously. "Oh Marcus, I'm so sorry. A woman claiming to be their mum took them just a few minutes ago. They're probably still in the car park," she said in a rush.

"What are you talking about?" Marcus glanced at Tiffany and noted her face was pale. She mumbled something and took off in the direction of the car park.

"What did she look like?" Marcus asked.

"Short black bob, art glasses, kind of immature."

A sudden chill froze his body before he bolted for the door and sprinted after Tiffany. As he ran, he wondered how the children had been released to someone without proof. That should never have happened.

"Mike! Polly!" Tiffany screamed in the middle of the car park. Church goers approached and asked what was happening, but she either didn't hear them or she simply ignored them.

Marcus scanned the car park. He knew Sally's car. A burgundy hatchback. He'd find it. He had to. There, turning onto the main road. The wheels screeched as she accelerated into the turn. He sprinted after it, but he was no match for a speeding car. As it disappeared from view, he whipped out his phone and called the police.

"My friend's children, kidnapped," he panted. Breathlessly, he gave the make of the car, license plate number, and Sally's name, to the operator.

He was still panting when Tiffany reached him. "Who's got them?" she asked frantically.

"It's a long story." He pulled her close and rubbed her back. "I've called the police. I'm sure they'll find them."

She pulled away. "But who took them, and why?" Her eyes flamed with anger.

"Her name's Sally Hubbard and she's been stalking me for several weeks."

"Why would she take my kids?" Tiffany was almost yelling.

"Because she's unstable." Marcus bit down hard on his lower lip. Why hadn't he done something about her? If he had, this wouldn't have happened. But how could he have anticipated she'd do something like this? He knew she was unstable, but not crazy enough to kidnap Tiffany's children. Jealousy. That was it. She was jealous. He recalled the strange words she'd spoken when she came to his office... *You just haven't realised that I'm the one for you. You haven't seen the love we could share, but I have. It's only a matter of time before you do, too. And when you do, you'll be begging for me to come back to you.*

He slipped an arm around Tiffany's shoulder. "Come on, let's walk back and I'll tell you everything."

AFTER THE POLICE arrived and took further details, Marcus drove Tiffany and his mother back to the estate. Some of Tiffany's anger had evaporated, leaving behind fear and confusion. Marcus had explained the woman's history, that she was the one responsible for his father's death, and that she'd become unstable after her time in jail. And that she believed she was in love with him.

The police had assured her they were doing everything possible to find the children, but back at the estate, Tiffany couldn't sit still and do nothing, so she began pacing.

"Tiffany, let's pray about this," Ruth said calmly. "God knows where the children are."

She stopped pacing. Of course. It was all so new for her that in her distraught state, she'd forgotten to pray. "That's a great idea." She joined Ruth and Marcus at the table. He took her hand and squeezed it. Ruth held out her hand for her to take, which she did.

"Let's pray," Ruth said. They all bowed their heads and she began. "Our dear Lord and Heavenly Father, we come to You in our time of need and ask that You be with those dear little children. If they're frightened, comfort them, if they're confused, let them know that You're with them. Wrap Your arms around them and pour Your peace into their hearts.

"And Lord, we pray also for Sally. Her mind is troubled. Let her see reason and return the children safely to Tiffany. Be with the police as they search for her and give them wisdom and clarity of mind. Lord God, we desperately need Your peace in this situation. Free us from our fears and let us trust in You. In Jesus' precious name we pray. Amen."

Tiffany let go of Ruth's hand and brushed tears from her eyes. "Thank you."

"You're more than welcome, dear." Smiling, she passed Tiffany a tissue and then spoke to Marcus. "Let's have some coffee while we wait."

Marcus stood and walked to the kitchen. Ruth wheeled closer to Tiffany and placed her hand lightly on her shoulder. "'God is our refuge and strength, an ever-present help in trouble. Therefore, we will not fear, though the earth give way and the mountains fall into the heart of the sea, though its waters roar and foam and the mountains quake with their surging.

The Lord Almighty is with us; the God of Jacob is our fortress.'"

Tiffany nodded and dabbed her eyes. She'd come to the realisation that God really did care, but she wasn't sure why He would have allowed a deranged woman to kidnap her children. Surely, He could have prevented that.

Ruth must have read her mind—something she was good at. "Being a Christian doesn't mean we won't have trials. But we know 'that in all things God works for the good of those who love Him, who have been called according to His purpose.' He will work this out for good, Tiffany. I'm sure of it."

Marcus returned with the coffee. As Tiffany took her first sip, Marcus's phone rang. Tiffany's body stiffened. She wanted desperately to believe it was good news, not bad.

Marcus picked up his phone and answered it.

Tiffany tried to listen, but she didn't have to. The expression on his face was all she needed. He nodded to her and smiled. After the call ended, he relayed the message. "They've got her, and the kids are fine. They want us to go to the station because the kids need to give a statement and they want you to be there."

Tiffany burst into tears.

Marcus wrapped her in his arms and hugged her. Eventually she asked in a very small voice, "And Sally?"

"She'll undergo a full psychiatric evaluation."

CHAPTER 25

"*P*olly! Mike!" Tiffany cried, crushing her children in a huge embrace, tears streaming down her cheeks.

"Mummy," Polly cried in reply. Mike remained quiet and slightly stiff. Tiffany knew he was trying to show how brave he'd been, while Polly let her fears run freely.

"She said you'd sent her to pick us up," Polly continued. "She knew our names and she knew yours. You always told us not to go with anyone who doesn't know our names. But she did."

"I know, sweetie, and I'm so sorry. I'm sorry I wasn't able to get there before she took you." Tiffany sniffed and tried to stop her tears. She held the children close, unwilling to let them go.

"Ms. Harris, I'm Officer Murray."

Looking up, she gave a tentative smile to the middle-aged officer with a kindly face.

"I know this is a difficult time, but I need you all to give a statement when you're ready."

Tiffany nodded. "Can you give us a moment?"

"Sure."

She sniffed again and then let the children go while she blew her nose. Marcus rubbed her back. It seemed such a natural thing for him to do under the circumstances, but the whole situation was quite surreal. After composing herself, she took the children's hands and ushered them into the interview room. Marcus followed along behind.

Listening to Mike and Polly explain to Officer Murray what had happened, Tiffany was relieved that nothing worse had occurred. The woman had been friendly and told the kids she was a friend of hers. She was going to take them to McDonald's and buy them lunch before taking them home.

But she didn't stop at the first McDonald's, or the second, or the third. That was when they grew scared. When they heard police sirens and the woman accelerated, they knew they were in trouble. Mike had held Polly's hand and tried to comfort her when she began to cry. The car skidded to a stop when a police car blocked their way, almost crashing into it. When the car stopped, the woman opened the door and fled, but an officer ran after her and caught her. She began screaming hysterically. It took two officers to control her.

"I'm so sorry you had to experience all of that," Marcus said to the children.

Tiffany was relieved they weren't injured and that they'd been found quickly. She hated to think what might have happened otherwise.

Marcus also gave a statement, but not within the children's hearing.

"What will happen to her, Mummy?" Polly asked as they waited for him.

"I'm not completely sure, darling, but she's sick, so she'll probably be taken to the hospital."

"She was nice to us at the start."

Tiffany was glad to hear that, but from what they'd told the officer, they'd become frightened when she sped up, and that made her angry. How dare the woman put her children at risk! What if she'd crashed the car? What had she hoped to gain by kidnapping her children? And how did she know who Tiffany and her children were in the first place. The woman had serious issues.

Marcus appeared soon after and drove them home. On the way, they stopped at McDonald's and Marcus said they could have whatever they wanted. It didn't compensate for what had happened, but it took their minds off the trauma for a short while.

When they arrived at Tiffany's home, she asked him if he'd like to come in. After what had happened, she was reluctant to be on her own. He agreed and helped her settle the children for a rest.

Sipping coffee with him at the kitchen table, she asked him to tell her more about Sally.

"We always sensed she was a little unhinged, and she spent some time in a psychiatric hospital not long after being released from jail. We assumed she'd gotten better, but she must have had a relapse. I should have contacted the police when I realised she was stalking me. What happened to your children today is my fault. I'm so sorry, Tiffany."

"You didn't know she was capable of such a thing. It's not your fault."

"That's kind of you to say that, but I feel responsible."

"If she has a psychiatric condition, that's not your fault."

"Perhaps not, but it seems that because of the accident, she's been living with guilt that apparently turned into an obsession. I should have stopped it."

"You can't change what happened. I've learned that. And the kids will be fine. Although I might get them some counseling, just to be sure." She had no idea how she'd pay for counseling, but figured she'd somehow come up with the money.

He must have read her mind, because he said, "That's a great idea, and I'll cover the cost."

His generosity and thoughtfulness overwhelmed her. Because of his financial status, the cost of counseling would be a drop in the bucket, but it was a kind gesture, nevertheless.

"Thank you."

SOON AFTER, he left with a promise to call to check how the children were later that afternoon. A tremendous void filled her heart as soon as he walked out the door, and she knew that despite her resolve never to become entangled with another man, Marcus Alcott had stolen her heart.

THE FOLLOWING DAY, Tiffany stayed home from work and kept the children from school. She called her mother and told her what had happened. Her mum was so upset she offered to come over right away.

Marcus called every second hour to check in. Around three in the afternoon, he called with an update. "Hi again." His gentle voice calmed Tiffany's heart. "Are you all still doing okay?"

"Yes, we're fine, thanks. Polly's taking another nap and Mike's watching a movie. My mum's still here."

"I'm glad. I thought I'd let you know that Sally went through her evaluation. Due to the stalking and kidnapping, she has been given a few diagnoses. They said she has a predisposition to Type One Bipolar Disorder and had been showing characteristics her whole life, but this was a severe psychotic episode."

"Oh, my goodness. So, this has been a long time coming?" Tiffany asked, horrified at the thought that Sally, a young woman with a treatable condition, had gotten so out of control.

"That's what it sounds like. She's been hospitalised and will receive a great deal of care and treatment. The officer said that her doctor is hopeful she'll recover, but she won't be released from the hospital until they're convinced she's stable which may be a long time. She'll probably be on medication for the rest of her life, and will also be charged with kidnapping."

Tiffany was glad to hear it, although it didn't calm her nerves entirely. She wished Sally the best and tried to let go of her anger, but she was still concerned about what could happen when she was released. The thought also crossed her mind that Sally could fake a recovery in order to be let out, but she decided not to focus on that. She'd been given new life in

Christ. Sally was being offered a new start by having her mental health condition treated. What if she could also come to know Christ and depend on Him as she recovered?

Everything within Tiffany wanted to beg God to never let Sally be released, to make her spend the rest of her life locked up. She wanted to ask Him to strike down anyone who would harm her family. She wanted to see the God of judgment in action.

But in the midst of her anger, she felt a still, small voice whispering to her. *Pray for her.*

Tiffany knew then. She had to pray for Sally. She had to ask God to take care of her and to bring her into His arms. She had to pray that Sally would come to know the peace that she herself was just discovering.

So, she would do just that. After ending the call with Marcus, she went into her room, got down on her knees, and asked God to show Sally His truth and to help her find new life in Him.

Tiffany knew that God would hear her prayers, even if they were implored in an attempt to calm her own spirit. She trusted Him to reveal Himself to Sally, and to soften her heart towards Him, but then it was up to her to respond.

When Marcus called again later in the evening, Tiffany was able to say that she finally was feeling better and that the kids were, too.

"I'm so glad, Tiffany," Marcus said. "I've been worried about you all day. Can I say once more how sorry I am?"

"You can, but I'm not upset with you. You couldn't have predicted what she'd do, and we're going to be okay," she replied, knowing that her statement was true. They *would* be okay. They *were* okay.

"I'm relieved to hear it, but I'd like to make it up to you."

"You don't need to do anything," she replied. "You've already offered to pay for counseling for the kids, which is already so generous."

"But I want to do more. I think you and the children could use a day without any stress. How does a day on my yacht sound?"

Tiffany smiled. Having already told him that their date on Friday would have to wait until she felt confident that the kids would feel safe without her, she was glad for the invitation. A day on his yacht with the children would give them the security of being together while allowing her and Marcus to enjoy one another's company. It sounded ideal. "You know, maybe I'm crazy, but I don't think any stalkers could follow us out on the water, so let's do it," she replied.

"Wonderful! Shall we book it in for Saturday?"

"That sounds perfect. I'll look forward to it, and I'm sure the children will too."

CHAPTER 26

*S*aturday couldn't come soon enough. The children were so excited to be spending a day on Marcus's yacht that they soon forgot about the episode with Sally. Tiffany deliberated what she should wear, never having been on a yacht before, but in the end she decided on a pair of white shorts, a hot-pink button-up blouse, a floppy hat and sandals. She packed her swimsuit and towels in case they stopped somewhere they could swim.

Marcus sent a car for them. He had some last-minute work to do with the new contract that couldn't wait or else he would have come himself. He apologised. She'd told him not to worry, it was okay. It wasn't the limo, but it was almost as fancy. The kids thought it was the poshest car they'd ever seen, but they hadn't been in the limo. When they arrived at the estate, Marcus was waiting for them. He was dressed in navy shorts and a white Tommy Hilfiger polo, looking every bit the sailor.

Her heart skittered when he took her hand and helped her out of the car. She smiled and thanked him.

"You look wonderful," he said, casting his gaze over her attire.

"I wasn't sure what to wear."

"It's perfect."

He walked with them to the jetty. She'd only seen the yacht from a distance, and as they came closer, she gasped. It was almost as big as the Manly ferry. "Do you sail this on your own?" she asked.

He chuckled. "No. There's a captain and a full crew aboard."

"Can I help?" Mike asked. Tiffany had to hold him back from running ahead.

"You sure can," Marcus replied.

He helped them board by way of a gangplank, and the captain, a young man by the name of Paul, smiled and welcomed them aboard 'Bree-ze'. Tiffany wondered if Marcus had named the boat after his wife, and assumed he had. She felt for him. It must be so hard having reminders of her everywhere.

The boat was amazing. It was a huge catamaran, and the cockpit was almost larger than her house. The white leather seats looked comfortable and enticing, a great place to sit and enjoy the view. But she couldn't see the children being happy to sit for long. She was relieved when Marcus offered to give them a full tour of the boat.

As they set off, the children sat with Paul and helped him steer while Tiffany and Marcus enjoyed coffee and croissants in the cockpit. The weather was perfect for a day on the harbour. The sun shone brilliantly, making the water sparkle.

A number of other yachts were taking advantage of the great weather, and soon the sails were up and they were sailing towards Little Manly across the harbour heads.

"Do you ever go out there?" Tiffany asked.

"I've been out a few times with Dave and some of the others from church. They love deep sea fishing."

"I'm not sure I'd be a fan of that!" She laughed. "Just crossing these heads is enough for me." Rollers were coming in from the ocean, and the boat rose and fell and made her feel a little squeamish.

"Are you okay?" he asked, reaching out his hand to squeeze hers.

"I'll be fine. I'm just not used to the rocking, that's all."

"Shall we go up front and get some fresh air?"

"Sure. I think that might help."

One of the crew collected their coffee cups and Marcus held her elbow as they walked to the front of the yacht. She was glad of his help since she could easily have lost her balance. Maybe one day she'd grow sea legs, but right now, she felt quite unsteady.

The fresh air helped, and as it whipped through her hair and sea water misted her face, she began to relax and enjoy not only the ride, but the company. She was very conscious of Marcus standing beside her, and she surprised herself by sidling closer and hoping he'd put his arm around her and was disappointed when he didn't. She chastised herself yet again for daydreaming about something that was not likely to ever happen.

The day turned out to be exactly what they needed. They anchored at Little Manly and the kids swam in the clear, blue water to their hearts' content. Paul lowered the jet ski that Tiffany didn't even know the boat was carrying, and Marcus took turns taking them each for rides. He offered to take Tiffany as well, and she almost refused, but at the last moment agreed, and she was so glad she did. Marcus told her to wrap her arms around his waist, which she had no hesitation doing. As they zoomed around the harbour, she laughed and laughed and couldn't have been happier.

On their return journey, while sitting in the cockpit, her eyes began to droop. The ocean had calmed a little since the morning, and after a full day in the sun and sea, it seemed that the tension of the past week had caught up with her and she succumbed. When she woke sometime later, she wondered where she was, but soon remembered when Marcus smiled at her.

"Did you have a good sleep?"

She nodded. "The best I've had in a long time."

"I'm glad. You looked so peaceful I didn't want to disturb you, but we're almost back."

She straightened and looked ahead. He was right. The yacht was approaching Marcus's jetty and Mike and Polly were helping one of the crew members with the ropes. Or sheets, as Marcus said they were called.

"It's been a lovely day. Thank you," she said.

"You're more than welcome. Let's do it again sometime soon."

She smiled. "I'd like that."

"And so would I."

. . .

144

THREE DAYS LATER, a parcel was sitting on the doorstep, addressed to Mike. Tiffany was puzzled. Mike never got parcels. "Can I open it?" he asked eagerly.

"Sure," she replied.

Mike carried it up the steps before tearing the paper off. "It's a pair of football boots!" he exclaimed. He proudly held them up.

Tiffany's eyes widened. Not only were they football boots, but they were the top brand she could never afford, given she couldn't even afford the cheapest brand. "Does it have a card?" she asked. But she already knew who they were from. Definitely not Steve. It had to be Marcus. But how did he know?

"I don't see one," Mike replied.

"Did you tell Marcus you needed boots when we were on the boat?"

He frowned. "I'm not sure. I might have. Can I try them on?"

"Yes. Go for it!"

The boots fit perfectly, and inside one, Mike found a note saying that his fees were paid. "Does that mean I can play?"

Tiffany smiled. "I guess so!" Although she could easily have been annoyed by Marcus's generosity, she wasn't, because he was a generous man with a big heart. Who could be annoyed by that?

OVER THE FOLLOWING WEEKS, Marcus surprised her again and again with spontaneous outings that they all enjoyed together. They got to know one another, and not only did Tiffany fall for his charm and kindly manner, but so did the kids. They loved all the outings that he took them on. Tiffany wanted to ask him to stop spoiling them, but after the way Steve treated them, she didn't have the heart to say anything since they were having such a wonderful time.

When she and Marcus finally had their first official date a few weeks later, Tiffany knew without a doubt that it was the first of many. He was the man of her dreams, a man after God's own heart. And as she grew in her relationship with the Lord, she saw more and more that He was the reason for the heart Marcus had.

That night, he booked a table at the fine dining restaurant on the top floor of Centrepoint Tower. She'd never been there, let alone eaten at the restaurant. After picking her up in the limo, they took the glass lift to the top. The ride was amazing, but not as amazing as the view. All of Sydney stretched before them. When Marcus stood behind her and slipped his arms around her waist, goosebumps covered her flesh.

"Are you cold?" he asked.

"No." But she snuggled against him and thought she was in seventh heaven when he nuzzled her neck with his lips. "I've been waiting for this moment for a long time," he whispered.

Closing her eyes, she let the joy of the moment fill her. She didn't pull away and longed for him to kiss her properly. She wished the lift would never stop, but when they reached the top, he removed his arms from her waist and placed his hand at the small of her back as the waiter greeted them and led them to their table.

The dinner was superb. She had the silver dory and clam chowder, served with kipfler potatoes and confit fennel, and he had the roasted paroo kangaroo loin with braised cabbage, sweet potato and coriander. After they finished eating, he asked if she fancied a walk along the beach. When she said she would, he called for the limo and asked the driver to take them to Coogee Beach.

After arriving, they removed their shoes and strolled along the beach arm in arm, and Tiffany couldn't think of a better way to end a perfect evening—until he stopped and turned to face her. His eyes were just visible in the moonlight, but in them she saw his heart. Tender, caring, loving. "I never expected to love another woman, but I'm falling for you, Tiffany." His voice was soft and as tender as his eyes. Her pulse raced. "No, that's not true," he continued. "I've already fallen for you. You've captured my heart, and I'd be the happiest man if you let me court you."

She almost laughed. Court her! She'd never expected to hear that! "Marcus, that's the sweetest thing I've ever heard! Of course you can court me."

He smiled. "Does that mean I can kiss you?"

"Yes, please! I never thought you'd ask!" Her heart beat double-time as he lowered his mouth and their lips met for the first time in a kiss that left her hungry for more.

That night, as she lay in bed, dreams of being courted by a billionaire played over and over in her mind, filling her with such warmth and anticipation that she could barely sleep.

CHAPTER 27

Three months had passed since their first official date, and Marcus was astounded at how Tiffany had grown in her relationship with the Lord during that time. Sometimes, when they were having dinner together, she'd bring up a theological topic he'd never looked into and ask him all sorts of deep questions.

Her curiosity and devotion challenged him in his own faith, forcing him to really consider some of the ways he looked at Scripture.

"Okay, but don't you see? Israel demanded a king. God warned them that they were being sinful and that *He* wanted to be their king. But He gave them a king anyway because they selfishly insisted on it," Tiffany pointed out one evening.

"So, you're suggesting that God gave in to their sinful demand?" he asked, confused.

"No, He used it for His own purposes. This is the same lineage that brought us Jesus, the true and final King!"

Tiffany exclaimed as they sat next to the pool while the kids swam.

Marcus suddenly saw the connection. He saw another instance of how God had taken sin and redeemed it for His own plans and purposes. It was right there in front of him, but he'd never thought about it like that.

"Tiffany, you amaze me. The way you keep studying Scripture is so encouraging and challenging," he told her, as he had many times in the previous months.

Mike and Polly were enjoying church, even going to Sunday school every week, now that they were confident Sally was never going to come back for them. And on Wednesdays, they went to kid's church while Tiffany was involved in the evening discipleship meetings.

But her favourite, she had told Marcus, was Ruth's Bible study. She'd been diligently attending and was learning a lot. And thanks to those women, she'd also been given a lot of book recommendations. Marcus knew how much she loved reading through all the material and learning about the Word of God from those who had been living the faith for many years.

She was growing into an incredibly strong Christian woman. And she'd also allowed herself to become vulnerable. When he'd first met her, although she was always polite to him, he knew she didn't trust him, or men in general.

She'd explained to him that her marriage to Steve had impacted her ability to trust any man, but she was working hard to overcome that. She had since made it clear that she trusted him, and that was all Marcus needed to know.

Her affection and the way she reciprocated his were

evidence that she would not be imprisoned in the cage of her former concerns. She was now free to live in grace and mercy, and there was no longer any need to put up walls to protect her heart.

"So, what do you think?" Marcus asked his mum one morning at breakfast.

Tears had sprung to her eyes. "You know what I think."

"Okay, but do you think it's a good idea? I know it's quick. Am I crazy to think about proposing to her so soon? With her past and everything she's gone through? And the fact that she still has trust issues. Am I sabotaging our future by wanting it to start now?"

"I think if she isn't ready, you'd know. You know full well that she'll say yes. You're wanting me to confirm what you already know and that's a waste of time. She loves you. She trusts you. Don't waste any more time," his mother said, patting his hand.

He was jubilant to gain his mother's approval. It was the encouragement he needed. With every passing day he spent with Tiffany, he'd grown more certain that he not only could love again, but that he did.

He'd spoken with his pastor about the challenges of falling in love again after losing Bree. And just like his mother had done, his pastor had urged him to move forward. "She's a wonderful woman, Marcus, and it's great to see you happy and in love after all these years of heartache. I wish you all the best."

Marcus not only loved Tiffany, he loved Mike and Polly as

well. He knew that he could be a father to them as much as they were willing to accept him as one.

Her family was also wonderful, constantly inviting him for gatherings at her parents' house. Her mother had hinted about the two of them having a future together. It seemed as though Marcus had everyone's approval. No matter how early it was in their relationship, everyone seemed to trust that they would make it.

He only had to hope that Tiffany felt that way. That she would trust him enough to accept his proposal and consent to a future with him.

Aware that it could destroy all of his plans, he finally decided to ask Tiffany's father if he would give his blessing.

"Have a seat, Marcus," Wayne insisted. He'd gone to the Watson's home later that same day, and now felt slightly anxious. *What if he didn't approve?*

"Thank you," Marcus said, easing himself into an old, worn armchair.

"When you called, it sounded important. What do you want to talk about?" Wayne asked.

Marcus let out a slow breath and clenched his hands together. "As you know, the past few months have been a whirlwind. From your daughter joining me as a friend for an event I needed a date for, to becoming someone I love very much, a lot has happened," Marcus began.

"Not to mention her kids getting kidnapped by your stalker..." Wayne added, lifting a brow.

Marcus looked at him sheepishly, knowing that it could be Wayne who distrusted him rather than Tiffany. After all, it was a woman obsessed with him who'd caused all the problems. And that meant he'd put Wayne's grandchildren in danger.

"Don't worry, Marcus, I'm not judging you for that," he said, grinning. "It's a father's job to put a little bit of fear in a man who comes around asking what I think you're about to ask. It doesn't change the fact that I'm going to approve."

Marcus exhaled in relief. "You're going to approve? But you don't know my question," Marcus said with a laugh.

"I think I do, but go ahead and ask it anyway," Wayne urged.

Marcus steadied himself. "I'd like to marry your daughter, Wayne."

"What a shock!" Wayne chuckled. "Are you here to tell me that or to ask for my approval?"

"I hope it's a little bit of both," Marcus replied.

"Then you get both. You have my approval, Marcus. You're a fine man and I like the way you look after my daughter. I appreciate the way you take care of Mike and Polly, and I'd be honoured to have you as part of our family. So please, feel free to ask Tiffany to marry you. She deserves some happiness after all she's been through."

Having received approval and confirmation from every side, all he had to do now was act on it. It was time to propose to Tiffany.

He prayed she'd trust him enough to say yes.

CHAPTER 28

$\mathcal{T}$iffany was thrilled to be dining out again with Marcus at yet another upmarket restaurant. Since they'd been dating, he'd been spoiling her, and she felt like a princess. Never before had she been treated so well by anyone, and despite her previously held conviction to remain totally independent, she was reveling in the attention.

That night they were dining at the 'Versailles Restaurant', a high-end French restaurant that had won award after award for its cuisine, service and ambience. Tiffany knew why. When they entered, it was like she was walking into a palace. Marcus told her that it had been designed to resemble the Palace of Versailles. They walked through parterre gardens with fountains and subtle lighting to reach the restaurant itself. Gold embellished statues filled every corner, and when they were shown to their table which overlooked the harbour, they were addressed in French. Luckily, Marcus could speak the language. She loved hearing him conversing with the waiter and wished she could speak French.

"Have you been to France?" she asked after they were seated.

"No, but I'd love to go one day and see the real palace." He reached out his hand and held hers, rubbing his thumb gently over her skin. Their gazes met and a tremor ran through her body. "And I'd love to go there with you."

She was wholly unprepared for that. France? With Marcus? Was he serious? "Really?" she asked, dumbfounded.

He nodded. "I can't think of anyone I'd rather see it with than you." His voice was calm, his gaze steady.

Her heart swelled at the thought of visiting France with him, but what were his intentions? It seemed too unbelievable to consider seriously. Plus, how could she go with him unless they were married? Suddenly she realised he might be planning to propose. She gulped and said, "That's very sweet of you. Of course, I'd love to visit France. Who wouldn't?"

After they finished eating, Marcus asked if she'd like to take a stroll along the harbour.

Tiffany smiled and nodded, thinking back to the night of the charity ball when this amazing journey had begun.

Walking with Marcus again along the harbour brought back memories of her life just five months ago. So much had changed in her heart. In the four months they'd been officially dating, Tiffany realised she'd become a different woman. She'd always believed that being vulnerable with a man would make her weak, but allowing Marcus to see the real her gave her confidence to be herself and made her strong. His respect for her was unlike anything she'd ever known before.

"Do you remember the first time we walked together?" Marcus asked. They were walking arm in arm and Tiffany had never felt more at peace.

"I was just thinking about the very same thing. How could I ever forget?" she replied.

"I so badly wanted to kiss you, or at least hold your hand that night," he confessed.

She chuckled. "And I was wishing you would. I was so mad at myself for wishing that, but I still thought it."

Stopping, he turned and faced her. Lowering his mouth, he brushed his lips across hers. "We need to make up for lost time." He pressed a little harder, and she kissed him back with a hunger that surprised her. She never wanted to leave the safety of his arms, but they were in public. She reluctantly pulled back. "What will people think?" she asked breathlessly.

He laughed. "I don't see any people, do you?"

She quickly glanced to the left and the right. "I guess not!"

He gazed into her eyes, and then cupping her cheeks with his hands, lowered his mouth again, pressing his lips gently against hers. This time, his kiss was slow and thoughtful and left her feeling like jelly.

After they broke the kiss, they continued walking until they reached the end of the pier where they sat on a bench seat. One other couple strolled arm in arm eating ice creams, and a few fishermen sat on the edge of the jetty, lines set, trying their luck. Marcus slipped his arm around her shoulder and pulled her closer when a cool breeze made her shiver. She snuggled in, laying her head on his shoulder and enjoying the closeness of his body.

They sat quietly, gazing out over the water. In the distance, the city lights lit up the night sky, but here in this secluded nook of the harbour, they could have been a world away from the bustling city. It was so peaceful, with only the sound of water gently lapping against the moored dinghies and the wooden legs of the pier, with the occasional noise of people laughing as they left the restaurant.

"You're an amazing woman, Tiffany," Marcus said in a soft voice. "And I love being amazed by you. In fact, I was thinking how nice it would be to spend the rest of my life being amazed by you."

Her heart began to pound. Was their conversation going to a place she'd both longed for yet still feared?

She lifted her head off his shoulder and looked into his eyes, wanting to read his intentions. She saw them clearly.

"Marcus..." she said, unable to prevent a coy grin growing on her face.

He shifted off the bench and onto one knee, taking her hands in his. "I know some people might think this is premature, but I don't care. I'm not just in love with you, Tiffany, I'm overwhelmed by you. In the short time we've had together, I've seen something exquisite and precious within your heart. I see the love of Christ in you, I see a woman who is seeking God, and I see a mother who loves her children fiercely."

Tiffany blinked back the tears pricking at her eyes.

He pulled a small box from his jacket pocket and opened it, holding it towards her. "I love you so much, Tiffany. I might have all the money a man could ever want or need, but it means nothing without someone special to share it with, and I'd love to share it with you. Tiffany, my love, I'd be the happiest man alive if you agree to be my wife."

Nodding through her tears, she threw her arms around his neck and breathed out a small, "Yes, of course I'll marry you. I love you with all my heart."

He kissed the nape of her neck and then pulled back and slowly slipped the exquisite diamond and sapphire ring onto her finger.

"It's gorgeous, Marcus. I love it!" She held her hand out to see it better. "Thank you." She smiled at him and thought her heart would explode with joy.

She'd been so hurt before, she never wanted to marry again. It had been something she'd fiercely determined long ago. She never wanted to be in a position of having to rely on a man, but Marcus wasn't like Steve or any other man she'd ever known. He was different. He was kind. He was generous. And she knew he would never hurt her.

He would always love his first wife, but Tiffany was coming to realise that his love for Bree didn't negate his love for her. He was giving his whole heart to her, and she wanted to give hers right back.

"Just so you know, I received permission from a lot of people. First, my own mum. Then your dad and your mum. And, remember yesterday when I picked up Mike and Polly from school?"

"You asked them?" Tiffany shrieked in laughter.

"I had to!" Marcus exclaimed.

"I can't believe they managed to keep it a secret!"

"They knew it would only be for a day. But yes, everyone has consented."

Tiffany felt a wave of peace wash over her as he pulled her tight and kissed her passionately. Since meeting Marcus, her life had changed irrevocably. And it was all she could have dreamed of and more.

CHAPTER 29

The day had finally arrived, and Marcus couldn't wait for Tiffany to become his wife. Standing at the end of the aisle, waiting for the music to start, he blew into his hands.

"It's okay, mate. She'll be here in a minute," Dave assured him. "Take a deep breath."

Nodding, he did what his friend suggested. There was no reason to be anxious, and he wasn't. He was simply filled with anticipation.

After settling himself, he mingled with the guests, greeting family and friends, but soon, it was time. He quickly hurried back to his position at the front when the music started, and everyone stood.

Polly entered first, sprinkling colourful flower petals from a small white basket, wearing a beautiful white princess-style dress. Her blonde hair fell around her shoulders and a crown of small daisies encircled her head. She looked so sweet.

When she reached him, he bent down and gave her hand a kiss. She then stood across from him, leaving enough room for the bridesmaid and Tiffany.

Mike came next, holding the rings on a white pillow. His hair was slicked back, and he wore a black suit with a tie that matched Marcus's. Marcus was so glad that the two of them had been getting along so well. Tiffany was thrilled that Mike finally had a man in his life who treated him with respect.

Denise, Tiffany's sister, entered next, and then came the moment he'd been waiting for. Marcus inhaled a deep breath.

When Tiffany entered on her father's arm, his breath hitched. He'd never seen anything so breathtaking. The strapless princess gown she wore was soft and feminine, and it suited her slim figure to a tee.

Her hair was in soft curls and her makeup was subtle, and perfect. When she reached him, Marcus could tell she was feeling confident, strong, and entirely ready for the commitment she was about to make. It was a moment he'd never forget.

The pastor welcomed everyone and then opened with prayer. They sang the hymns they'd chosen together, 'Great is Thy Faithfulness' and 'Love Divine All Loves Excelling.' Both hymns contained lyrics that meant so much to them.

Finally, the time came for them to say their vows. Marcus took Tiffany's hand in his and met her gaze. "Tiffany, I'm far from perfect and my love is far from perfect, but I vow to pursue God faithfully so that I can be a husband to you like Hosea. The love described in the book of the same name is one of deep, selfless affection and pursuit.

"I vow to make it my goal to love you like Hosea loved his

bride, and to lead you with cords of kindness, and with bands of love."

Although her eyes moistened, she smiled earnestly and began hers, looking deeply into his eyes. "Marcus, thank you for pursuing me as Christ pursues the church. Thank you for loving me as Hosea loved his bride. I promise to love and cherish you, for better or for worse, for richer or poorer, in sickness and in health, until death do us part, according to God's holy ordinance, and thereto I pledge myself to you."

He felt a bottomless peace and satisfaction. God had given him a second chance at love, and he'd grasped it with both hands. While he'd never forget Bree, his future was with Tiffany, and he loved her more than words could ever express.

After they exchanged rings and the pastor pronounced them man and wife, he lifted her veil and gazed into her eyes before kissing her with passion and longing.

The reception was held on the grounds of the estate. They'd considered other venues, but none were as perfect as their very own place, with the dazzling harbour as the backdrop. As they mingled with their guests, enjoying delicious canapes and drinks, Marcus was unable to take his eyes off his bride. She was drop-dead gorgeous, and love for her swelled inside him until it hurt.

For them both, this day was the beginning of their new life together. He couldn't wait for the days ahead, but he relished the present. This day, their wedding day, was a day of commitment and joy.

Later, as the reception came to a close, they waved goodbye to their friends and family and climbed into the limo, the very same one that had taken them to the charity ball all those months before. Marcus had chosen an exclusive six-star hotel in the city centre for their first night together as husband and wife. He'd booked the penthouse, and when they arrived, they were greeted like royalty. News must have leaked out that he was getting married, because a row of photographers snapped shot after shot as they walked from the limo to the hotel foyer.

Tiffany turned to him and laughed. "I've never been famous before!"

He laughed with her and kissed the side of her head. When they reached the penthouse, he pulled her close and gazed into her eyes, brushing wispy strands of hair off her face with his fingers. "Well, Mrs. Alcott, at last we're alone." Desire swept through him, and he lowered his mouth and kissed her the way he'd desired since the night of the ball, before gathering her in his arms and carrying her to the king-sized bed.

The next morning, when Marcus woke and gazed at Tiffany's sleeping form beside him, he'd never been as content and as happy as in that moment. The thought that he would wake up beside her each morning for the rest of their lives filled him with joy.

Her eyes flickered and she grinned at him. "Good morning!"

"And good morning to you, my love." He slipped his arms around her shoulder and brushed her lips lightly with his. "I love you so much, Tiffany. And you look even more gorgeous with tousled hair." He chuckled as he showered her lips and jaw with kisses.

"And you don't look too bad, either," she whispered between kisses.

A little later they ordered room service and enjoyed a delicious continental breakfast while gazing out at the city and the harbour, which was as blue and sparkling as the sapphire in Tiffany's ring.

But they didn't have long before they needed to leave for the airport.

"I'm so excited," Tiffany said as they packed their bags.

Her excitement delighted him. Although their honeymoon would be shorter than he would have liked, there was good reason. For two weeks, he and Tiffany would enjoy a secluded chalet in Hawaii with no one to distract them, but following that, Mike and Polly were joining them for another two weeks in Italy and France.

DURING THEIR TWO weeks in Hawaii, they went to the beach every morning and enjoyed the sun and the surf. But most of the time they spent alone in their exclusive chalet where they had everything they needed.

One evening towards the end of their honeymoon, they sat together on the sand watching the sun set, and Marcus asked her if she was happy.

She looked at him as if he were crazy and then grinned. "I've never been happier in my life."

"Me either." Pulling her close, he kissed her passionately.

THE FOLLOWING DAY they flew back to Sydney and swooped up Mike and Polly for the whole family honeymoon.

The next two weeks were spent in Italy and France, seeing amazing sights and eating wonderful food. Polly was amazed by the Eiffel Tower and Mike wanted to spend the whole vacation at the Colosseum so he could pretend to be fighting battles.

But the most amazing place for Tiffany was the Palace of Versailles. She'd never seen such splendour and beauty, but most importantly, Marcus had kept his promise, and for that, she loved him to bits.

The sum of the trip was the knowledge that they had an entire future to spend together, to love one another and to serve God.

Each morning they determined with every breath, every kiss, and every moment, to give God the glory for bringing them together and for giving them both a second chance at love.

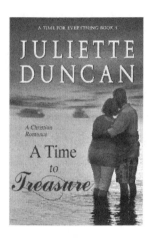

A Time to Treasure

<u>Prologue</u>

"There is a time for everything,
and a season for every activity under the heavens:
a time to be born and a time to die,
a time to plant and a time to uproot,
a time to kill and a time to heal,
a time to tear down and a time to build,
a time to weep and a time to laugh,
a time to mourn and a time to dance,
a time to scatter stones and a time to gather them,
a time to embrace and a time to refrain from embracing,
a time to search and a time to give up,
a time to keep and a time to throw away,
a time to tear and a time to mend,
a time to be silent and a time to speak,
a time to love and a time to hate,
a time for war and a time for peace."

Ecclesiastes 3:1-8

Chapter One

Sydney, Australia

Wendy Miller rigidly held her tears in check when her eldest daughter, Natalie, slipped on her beautiful wedding gown. The strapless A-line style suited Natalie's slim figure perfectly, but the prospect of her daughter walking down the aisle without her father brought a massive lump to Wendy's throat.

Wendy's husband, Greg, had suffered a fatal heart attack four years earlier, and although the pain she felt whenever she thought of him had lessened to a dull ache, it was moments like these that brought it rushing back.

"How does it look, Mum?" Natalie stood in front of the full-length mirror, peering over her shoulder at the back of the gown, while Roxanne, the gown's creator, made some minor adjustments.

"It's perfect, sweetheart. You're going to be a gorgeous bride."

Relief filled Natalie's face. "Thank you."

"Your father would have been so proud to walk you down the aisle in this," Wendy added in a wistful tone.

"Mum! You need to stop saying that. It's hard enough as it is."

Wendy bit her lip. Natalie was right. They were both struggling, and Natalie didn't need constant reminders that her father wouldn't be there on her special day when it no doubt was on her mind anyway. Wendy reached out and rubbed Natalie's arm. "I know, sweetheart, I'm sorry."

Natalie stood completely still while Roxanne inspected the gown, making the odd adjustment here and there. Dressed in an oversized multi-coloured loose-fitting shirt, purple tights and yellow sneakers, the young woman didn't look like one of Sydney's top fashion designers, but Roxanne Alexander was a multi-award winner eagerly sought after by the well-to-do, and they'd been fortunate to engage her services. "I won't do the final adjustments until the week before the wedding, but other than that, I think it's done," Roxanne said as she straightened.

Natalie beamed. "I love it so much. Thank you. Now all I have to do is eat salad for the next three months."

Roxanne laughed. "I wouldn't worry about that. A few extra pounds won't matter."

"Great! I wasn't looking forward to starving myself."

Wendy chuckled. Her daughter was as thin as a rake, even though she had a voracious appetite. "I don't think there's any chance of that. Come on, get dressed and I'll buy you lunch."

While Roxanne helped Natalie out of the gown, Wendy inspected the bridesmaids' dresses, which Roxanne also had designed. Paige, Wendy's youngest daughter, had been less than co-operative and showed little interest in her sister's wedding, turning up only once for a fitting. Wendy sometimes wondered if she'd even turn up for the wedding. She sighed heavily. It wasn't helpful comparing her children, but Natalie and Paige were so different. And then there was Simon…

"See you next time." Roxanne waved as Wendy and Natalie headed for the door.

"We'll look forward to it." Wendy smiled and then followed Natalie to the lift. While they waited, Wendy slipped her arm around Natalie's waist. "I'm sorry I get teary so often. It's… well, you know?"

"It's okay Mum. I understand. I wish Dad was here, too."

"I know you do, sweetheart."

The lift arrived and the doors opened. Stepping inside, they rode down the four levels, emerging into the foyer of the high-end building in downtown Sydney.

"Where would you like to go?" Wendy asked.

Natalie shrugged. "I don't mind, your choice."

"Okay. I know just the place." Wendy linked her arm through Natalie's and together they headed out into the bustling city. Taxis honked, moving like snails through the congested streets. Shoppers strolled along the footpath, chatting, pausing to look in shop windows, oblivious of the office workers weaving around them, hurrying to grab a quick mid-day meal before returning to their respective offices for the afternoon.

The aroma of freshly baked pizza wafted from an Italian restaurant, mingling with the scent of hot dogs piled high on a vendor's cart at the corner of Edward and King. "I wouldn't mind pizza," Natalie remarked, looking longingly over her shoulder while they waited for the lights to change.

"That's not really what I had in mind," Wendy said.

"What's wrong with pizza?"

Wendy laughed. "Nothing. Nothing at all. You know how much I love Italian food. I was just thinking of your waistline and your wedding dress." Wendy paused and then leaned in close to her daughter. "To be quite honest, I'm mostly worried about the mother-of-the-bride dress!"

The lights changed and Natalie giggled as they joined the

crush of pedestrians crossing to the other side. They walked on in comfortable silence, Natalie seemingly content to follow Wendy, and several minutes later, they arrived at one of Wendy's favourite restaurants. One she and Greg had dined at often. Maybe it wasn't the wisest choice, but she couldn't think of a nicer place to lunch with her daughter.

When the maître d' greeted them, Wendy asked for an outdoor table.

"Of course, Mrs. Miller, follow me," the smartly dressed young woman replied.

Natalie raised a brow at her mother and walked beside her to the table on the balcony that the maître d' chose for them. After the young woman settled them in and promised to send a waiter to take their orders, Natalie leaned forward. "We didn't have to come here, Mum. It'll cost a fortune!"

"It's okay, darling. I wanted to spoil you," Wendy replied, trying hard to keep her voice steady. The restaurant had one of the best views of the harbour and the Opera House, and on this perfect spring day, the water glistening in the sunshine was just glorious. Just like the days when she and Greg came here…

"You don't need to," Natalie replied. She grew silent for a few seconds, her face paling. Grabbing Wendy's arm, she asked, "Are you okay, Mum?"

Wendy frowned. "Of course I am. What makes you think I'm not?"

"You look tired, that's all. And bringing me here…" Natalie's voice trailed away, but Wendy could see fear in her daughter's eyes.

"You wonder if I'm sick?"

"Yes."

Wendy squeezed Natalie's hand. "I'm fine. Nothing to worry about. Honestly."

"Are you sure?" Natalie asked, frowning.

"Positive!"

A male waiter approached and stopped beside the table. The two women grabbed their menus and quickly perused them.

"Are you ready to order, ladies, or shall I come back?" the well-groomed, dark-haired young man asked politely.

"Could you give us a few minutes, please?" Wendy removed her designer sunglasses and smiled at him.

"Of course." He poured two glasses of water from the jug on the table and stepped aside.

"There's no pizza on the menu," Natalie whispered loudly.

Wendy laughed. "You don't need pizza, Natalie."

"I know." Natalie chuckled. "Shall we share the paella instead?"

Wendy set her menu on the table and smiled lovingly at her daughter. "Good choice." She waved the waiter over and placed the order. After he left, she slipped her sunglasses back on, sipped her water, and studied her daughter. What would she do without Natalie? Soon, her eldest daughter would be married and have less time to spend with her mother. The thought saddened Wendy, but she knew she had to deal with it. She couldn't, but more importantly, wouldn't, impose on Natalie and Adam. The first year of marriage was such a special time. Even now, after all the years that had passed, memories of her first year with Greg filled her with such warmth. They'd had a wonderful marriage. But it was no good constantly reminiscing. Although he'd be waiting for her in the life to come, he was gone from this earth, and she had to accept that fact and try to build a new life on her own.

"Have you spoken to Simon lately?" Natalie asked.

Wendy blinked and returned her attention to Natalie. "Not for a few weeks. He's replied to a few texts, but I think he's super busy with work. Did you know he got a promotion?"

Natalie frowned again. "No. He's always busy when I call. Makes me think he doesn't want to talk to me anymore."

"You know your brother. When he doesn't want to talk, he doesn't want to talk. But when he chooses to, you can't stop him."

"Yes, but surely he can find time to talk to *you* at least once a week. You're his mother, after all."

"I've come to the conclusion that we have to give him space," Wendy replied as positively as she could, because, the truth was, she also wondered why Simon found it so hard to keep in touch, but she *was* his mother, and she wouldn't speak ill of him with his sister.

Natalie crossed her arms. "If he keeps this up much longer, I'm going to drive to his house and make him talk. I mean it!"

"Don't be like that, sweetheart. He doesn't like it when we pressure him, you know that."

"I don't understand him! You'd think with Dad gone, he'd be more attentive of you."

"I can look after myself. But I agree, it'd be lovely to see more of him."

The waiter approached and set the paella on the table between them. "Would you like me to serve?" he asked.

Wendy flashed an appreciative smile. "We'll be fine, thanks. It smells wonderful."

The waiter nodded, refilled their glasses, and wished them *bon appétit* before leaving them to their meal.

"Pass your plate, Mum," Natalie said, holding her hand out.

Wendy complied and Natalie heaped several spoons of the colourful dish onto the middle of the plate. Wendy held her hand up. "That's plenty, darling. Thank you."

"Are you sure? There's a lot here."

"Yes, that's fine."

Natalie filled her plate and then quickly scooped a huge spoonful into her mouth, releasing a pleasurable sigh. Wendy was glad the conversation about Simon had been dropped. His lack of communication did worry her, and she often wondered if something was wrong, but didn't want Natalie concerned about him with her wedding fast approaching. Wendy decided to call him again when she got home.

After making quick work of the paella, Natalie leaned back in her chair and placed her hands across her stomach. "So, what have you decided about the trip?"

Wendy sipped her iced tea and released a long sigh. Greg's grandmother, who lived just south of London, was turning ninety, and Wendy had booked a trip to the U.K. to attend the celebration. She'd also invited her friend, Robyn, to accompany her, but now Robyn couldn't go because her mother had taken ill, and Wendy was considering cancelling. She set her glass on the table and toyed with her fork. "I don't think I'll go."

"Oh Mum, I think you should. Since Dad's death, you've hardly taken a holiday—I think it'll do you good."

"But on my own?"

Natalie chuckled. "You never know, you might meet a handsome gentleman who'll sweep you off your feet!"

"Natalie!"

"Sorry…" A playful grin had spread across Natalie's face. She leaned forward, crossing her arms on the table. "Seriously, I think you should go. You've travelled a lot, you'll be fine. You need to go, Mum."

Wendy sighed heavily. "I'll give it some more thought. If I stay home, I can help more with the wedding preparations."

"You've already done more than enough. It's all in hand," Natalie replied with just a hint of exasperation in her voice.

"I know. But it seems strange to think of travelling to the other side of the world without your dad. It won't be the same."

Natalie squeezed her mother's hand. "I know. But go. Do it for Dad."

Wendy grimaced and swallowed the lump in her throat. "I'll think about it, but right now, I think I'd like coffee. Would you like one?"

"That would be lovely. Thank you."

Wendy beckoned the waiter over and ordered two cups.

"And can I tempt you with the dessert menu?" He quirked a brow as he held out two.

Wendy smiled politely. "Thank you, but no. Coffee will be fine."

Natalie leaned forward again after the waiter left, her face filled with disappointment. "I was going to order something," she said in a sulky tone.

Wendy chuckled, shaking her head. "You do take after your father with your sweet tooth."

"I can't help it," Natalie replied defensively, but then she laughed.

"I guess not. But even though Roxanne said it didn't matter, you should still watch what you're eating." Wendy quickly bit her lip. She shouldn't have said that. Natalie was a grown woman and could make her own decisions about what to eat and what to avoid. Thank goodness Natalie had an understanding nature. Paige would never have let her get away with saying anything like that. "I'm sorry darling. Have whatever you want." Wendy smiled and beckoned the waiter again.

~

CEDAR SPRINGS RANCH, TEXAS

Bruce McCarthy swung his legs off the bed and glanced at his watch. *Three p.m.* Releasing a slow breath, he ran his hand over his still thick, but graying hair. He really had to stop falling asleep in the afternoons—it was such a waste of time. However, now his eldest son, Nate, was running the ranch and insisted he take it easy, Bruce often found his eyes drooping in the early afternoon following their substantial mid-day meal, and he usually succumbed to a nap. However, he wasn't tired—he was just bored.

At sixty-three years of age, Bruce wasn't old, but his brush with bowel cancer a year earlier had shaken his sons, especially Nate. Although he'd beaten the disease, Nate had placed him on light duties, but Bruce was bored to tears. Retirement didn't suit him. He'd much rather be out tending cattle instead of looking after the books, which had never been one of his strong points.

A tentative knock sounded on the door. "Dad..." It was Nate, whispering in a low voice.

"Come in, son." Bruce pushed to his feet and crossed the room, grabbing a bottle of water from a small refrigerator tucked in a corner.

The door opened and Nate poked his rugged, good-looking cowboy head inside. "I'm heading to the bank in a few minutes. Need anything?"

Bruce shook his head. "I'm fine, thanks. I'm going to town soon, anyway."

Nate's forehead creased. "Sure you're up to it?"

Bruce did his best to hide his annoyance at his son's remark. He didn't need molly-coddling—the doctor had given him a clean bill of health. If only Nate wouldn't worry so much. And it was only a meeting at church to discuss fund-raising for the upgrade of the children's ministry hall. He wasn't about to do the actual renovations. "Of course I'm up to it," he replied with a reassuring smile before taking a slug of water. He didn't mention to Nate the other thing he was doing in town. He'd save that for later, when it was all sorted and too late to do anything about.

After Nate closed the door, Bruce sat at his desk and opened the drawer, taking out the itinerary the young woman at the travel agency had drawn up for him a few days earlier. He'd sworn her to secrecy. If Nate knew he was planning a trip to Ireland and England on his own, Bruce knew it was unlikely he'd even reach the airport lounge, let alone board the plane. But could he do it? He'd always thought that when he retired, he and his wife, Faith, would travel the world together, but Faith had passed on ten years earlier. Now, the choice was to go on his own or not at all.

Bruce re-read the itinerary. First stop, Ireland, the land of his forebears. His grandfather, Edward Bruce McCarthy, emigrated from Ireland in his early twenties, bought Cedar Springs Ranch and never returned. However, he never forgot his homeland and told endless tales and stories about the beautiful green isle. Ireland, Edward had told his young grandson, was a land filled with poets and fables, dreamers and agitators. Edward had sown a seed in the young Bruce's mind, and he wanted to see it for himself. He'd recently decided that now was the perfect time to visit the land he'd heard so much about, and maybe try to find some family members at the same time.

To Bruce it made perfect sense to go. He wasn't needed on the ranch, and after his health scare, every day was a blessing, and he wanted to make the most of the precious gift of life. Yes, he'd do it. He'd make the booking, pay for it, and then tell the family.

After dropping Natalie outside her apartment block, Wendy continued on to her home at Cremorne, a suburb on the northern side of Sydney Harbour. It still was, and always had been, a lovely family home. She and Greg bought it soon after they married and had raised their children there. However, the memories could sometimes be overwhelming and the sprawling three-level home with views over the glistening harbour seemed so big and quiet now that only she and Paige lived there. But since Paige was rarely at home, it was almost as if Wendy lived alone, and that made the house seem even larger and emptier.

She turned her car into the driveway, waved to Rose, her elderly neighbour who looked up from her gardening and smiled, and then drove into the double garage. Stepping out of the car, the boxes stacked against one side of the garage wall caught Wendy's attention. Simon's… She let out a sigh. Would he ever collect them? She'd given him several ultimatums but hadn't the heart to follow through with tossing his things out when he hadn't come for them by the appointed date. She sighed again and unlocked the internal door leading to the house. It didn't matter. It wasn't as if the space was being used for anything else. Paige didn't have a car, and Wendy had finally sold Greg's large SUV just last year, so there really was no need to hassle Simon.

Pushing the door open, Wendy stepped into the house, set her bag on the kitchen counter, and filled the kettle. A faint meow sounded from the sunroom, and moments later, Muffin, Wendy's large, fluffy Persian, rubbed against her legs. Wendy bent down and picked him up, gave him a cuddle, and then set him back on the floor while she made a cup of tea.

After turning on some background music to cover the silence that always filled the rambling house these days, she carried her tea to the sunroom and sat in her favourite chair. Muffin immediately joined her and settled on her lap.

Opening the book she'd begun the night before, Wendy began reading while sipping her tea. She soon closed it when she found herself re-reading the same paragraph several times. Her focus was elsewhere. Having all but decided to cancel the trip to London, the conversation with Natalie now had her mind awhirl. Maybe she should go. Could Natalie be right, that it might do her good? Her gaze travelled to the large family photo on the far wall, taken not long before Greg passed away unexpectedly. They all looked so happy, and they *had* been. Such a different story now. Paige hadn't coped well with her father's sudden death and blamed God for letting him die before his time. Simon had withdrawn further. Natalie did what she always did and soldiered on. They all had their own ways of coping. Wendy drew comfort and strength from quiet times spent in the Word, her family, her church, and her work as a part-time University Lecturer. But she still missed Greg terribly. She guessed she always would.

She reached for the travel pack the agent had given her and flicked through the itinerary. She and Robyn had planned to visit Ireland before flying to England. Greg had always wanted to visit the emerald isle. Wendy wasn't sure what had sparked his interest, but he'd always promised they'd go, and she'd been looking forward to seeing it. But could she do it on her own? Would it make her miss him more, or would it help her let go and move on? She drew a deep breath and closed her eyes, fingering the cross around her neck. *Lord, I'm really struggling with this—please show me what to do. You know how much I miss Greg, and how heavy my heart is when I think about travelling to the other side of the world without him, but maybe I should go. Please help me draw strength from You, and please guide and direct me. In Jesus' precious name. Amen.*

Half an hour later, after finishing her tea and finally finishing a chapter of her book, inexplicable peace flooded Wendy's heart. She made up her mind. She'd go to the birthday party in London, and to Ireland. She'd do it for Greg, but also for herself. She needed to start making a life for herself without him, because deep down, she knew that the loneliness that was her constant companion wouldn't leave until she did. Clinging to memories, as wonderful as they were, wouldn't help her move forward. Taking this trip, no matter how challenging it might be, would be a start to building a new life. Drawing a resolved breath, she picked up the phone and called the travel agent.

Grab your copy and continue reading by going to www.juliettedunca.com/library.

A Time for Everything Series

A Time For Everything Series is a mature-age contemporary Christian romance series set in Sydney, Australia and Texas, USA. If you like real-life characters, faith-filled families, and friendships that become something more, then you'll love these inspirational second-chance romances.

The True Love Series

Set in Australia, what starts out as simple love story grows into a family saga, including a dad battling bouts of depression and guilt, an ex-wife with issues of her own, and a young step-mum trying to mother a teenager who's confused and hurting. Through it all, a love story is woven. A love story between a caring God and His precious children as He gently draws them to Himself and walks with them through the trials and joys of life.

"A beautiful Christian story. I enjoyed all of the books in this series. They all brought out Christian concepts of faith in action."

"Wonderful set of books. Weaving the books from story to story. Family living, God, & learning to trust Him with all their hearts."

The Precious Love Series

The Precious Love Series continues the story of Ben, Tessa and Jayden from the The True Love Series, although each book can be read on its own. All of the books in this series will warm your heart and draw you closer to the God who loves and cherishes you without condition.

"I loved all the books by Juliette, but those about Jaydon and Angie's stories are my favorites...can't wait for the next one..."

"Juliette Duncan has earned my highest respect as a Christian romance writer. She continues to write such touching stories about real life and the tragedies, turmoils, and joys that happen while we are living. The words that she uses to write about her characters relationships with God can only come from someone that has had a very close & special with her Lord and Savior herself. I have read all of her books and if you are a reader of Christian fiction books I would highly recommend her books." Vicki

∾

The Shadows Series

An inspirational romance, a story of passion and love, and of God's inexplicable desire to free people from pasts that haunt them so they can live a life full of His peace, love and forgiveness, regardless of the circumstances. Book 1, *"Lingering Shadows"* is set in England, and follows the story of Lizzy, a headstrong, impulsive young lady from a privileged background, and Daniel, a roguish Irishman who sweeps her off her feet. But can Lizzy leave the shadows of her past behind and give Daniel the love he deserves, and will Daniel find freedom and release in God?

Hank and Sarah - A Love Story, *the Prequel to "The Madeleine Richards Series" is a FREE thank you gift for joining my mailing list. You'll also be the first to hear about my next books and get exclusive sneak previews. Get your free copy at www.julietteduncan.com/subscribe*

The Madeleine Richards Series

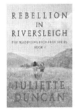  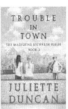 

Although the 3 book series is intended mainly for pre-teen/ Middle Grade girls, it's been read and enjoyed by people of all ages.

"Juliette has a fabulous way of bringing her characters to life. Maddy is at typical teenager with authentic views and actions that truly make it feel like you are feeling her pain and angst. You want to enter into her situation and make everything better. Mom and soon to be dad respond to her with love and gentle persuasion while maintaining their faith and trust in Jesus, whom they know, will give them wisdom as they continue on their lives journey. Appropriate for teenage readers but any age can enjoy." Amazon Reader

The Potter's House Books...stories of hope, redemption, and second chances. Find out more here:

http://pottershousebooks.com/our-books/

The Homecoming

Kayla McCormack is a famous pop-star, but her life is a mess. Dane Carmichael has a disability, but he has a heart for God. He had a crush on her at school, but she doesn't remember him. His simple faith and life fascinate her, but can she surrender her life of fame and fortune to find true love?

Unchained

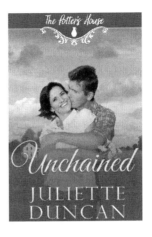

Imprisoned by greed – redeemed by love

Sally Richardson has it all. A devout, hard-working, well-respected husband, two great kids, a beautiful home, wonderful friends. Her life is perfect. Until it isn't.

When Brad Richardson, accountant, business owner, and respected church member, is sentenced to five years in jail, Sally is shell-shocked. How had she not known about her husband's fraudulent activity? And how, as an upstanding member of their tight-knit community, did he ever think he'd get away with it? He's defrauded clients, friends, and fellow church members. She doubts she can ever trust him again.

Locked up with murderers and armed robbers, Brad knows that the only way to survive his incarceration is to seek God with all his heart - something he should have done years ago. But how does he convince his family that his remorse is genuine? Will they ever forgive him?

He's failed them. But most of all, he's failed God. His poor decisions have ruined this once perfect family.

They've lost everything they once held dear. Will they lose each other as well?

Blessings of Love

She's going on mission to help others. He's going to win her heart.

Skye Matthews, bright, bubbly and a committed social work major, is the pastor's daughter. She's in love with Scott Anderson, the most eligible bachelor, not just at church, but in the entire town.

Scott lavishes her with flowers and jewellery and treats her like a lady, and Skye has no doubt that life with him would be amazing. And yet, sometimes, she can't help but feel he isn't committed enough. Not to her, but to God.

She knows how important Scott's work is to him, but she has a niggling feeling that he isn't prioritising his faith, and that concerns her. If only he'd join her on the mission trip to Burkina Faso...

Scott Anderson, a smart, handsome civil engineering graduate, has just received the promotion he's been working for for months. At age twenty-four, he's the youngest employee to ever hold a position of this calibre, and he's pumped.

Scott has been dating Skye long enough to know that she's 'the one', but just when he's about to propose, she asks him to go on mission with her. His plans of marrying her are thrown to the wind.

Can he jeopardise his career to go somewhere he's never heard of, to work amongst people he'd normally ignore?

If it's the only way to get a ring on Skye's finger, he might just risk it...

And can Skye's faith last the distance when she's confronted with a truth she never expected?

Stand Alone Christian Romantic Suspense

Leave Before He Kills You

When his face grew angry, I knew he could murder...

That face drove me and my three young daughters to flee across Australia.

I doubted he'd ever touch the girls, but if I wanted to live and see them grow, I had to do something.

The plan my friend had proposed was daring and bold, but it also gave me hope.

My heart thumped. What if he followed?

Radical, honest and real, this Christian romantic suspense is one woman's journey to freedom you won't put down…get your copy and read it now.

ABOUT THE AUTHOR

Juliette Duncan is a Christian fiction author, passionate about writing stories that will touch her readers' hearts and make a difference in their lives. Although a trained school teacher, Juliette spent many years working alongside her husband in their own business, but is now relishing the opportunity to follow her passion for writing stories she herself would love to read. Based in Brisbane, Australia, Juliette and her husband have five adult children, eight grandchildren, and an elderly long haired dachshund. Apart from writing, Juliette loves exploring the great world we live in, and has travelled extensively, both within Australia and overseas. She also enjoys social dancing and eating out.

Connect with Juliette:

Email: juliette@julietteduncan.com

Website: www.julietteduncan.com

Facebook: www.facebook.com/JulietteDuncanAuthor

Twitter: https://twitter.com/Juliette_Duncan

Made in the USA
Lexington, KY
11 December 2019

58450286R00109